THE ALIGNMENT ECHO III

The Alignment Network

Mark Anderson, PhD

Probe — Planet — Galaxy

THE ALIGNMENT ECHO III: ***The Alignment Network***
Mark Anderson, PhD
Probe — Planet — Galaxy

Copyright

This is a work of fiction. Names, characters, places, events, organizations, technologies, and incidents are either products of the author's imagination or are used fictitiously. Any resemblance to actual persons, living or dead, events, or entities is purely coincidental.

Cover Image: Artwork generated with artificial intelligence.
The colors humans paint onto galaxies are not illusions. They are data translations that turn invisible physics into something the human eye can finally see.

First Edition

Printed in the United States of America

ISBN: 979-8-9949357-5-0 (ebook)
ISBN: 979-8-9949357-6-7 (paperback)

Disclaimer

This science-fiction novel incorporates scientific concepts, historical references, astronomical phenomena, and space-exploration milestones for narrative purposes. While grounded in established research where possible, the interpretations, extrapolations, technologies, and scenarios presented are speculative.

Nothing in this work should be construed as technical instruction, scientific guidance, or predictive claim.

Dedication

For those who believe
that patience is a form of intelligence,
and that restraint can carry meaning farther
than speed ever could.

Acknowledgments

This book exists because of curiosity — shared, challenged, and refined.

Thank you to the scientists, linguists, engineers, historians, and explorers whose real work continues to expand our understanding of the universe. Their discoveries remind us that exploration is not only about reaching farther, but about learning how to ask better questions.

Thank you to readers who value quiet tension, thoughtful discovery, and stories that trust intelligence more than spectacle.

With gratitude to the engineers and dreamers who launched Voyager 1 (September 5, 1977) and Voyager 2 (August 20, 1977), in pursuit of space exploration.

And gratitude to the many researchers, space agencies, and scientific communities around the world whose dedication to discovery continues to shape humanity's future.

Some doors open only when we stop trying to force them.

Table of Contents

Copyright 2

Disclaimer 2

Dedication 3

Acknowledgments 3

Table of Contents 4

Preface 7

Dramatis Personae 8

Prologue: The First Light 10

Chapter 1: The Signal That Answered 13

Chapter 2: The Geometry of Seven 19

Chapter 3: The First Response 26

Chapter 4: The Spiral Equation 35

Chapter 5: The Central Signal 44

Chapter 6: The Linguist 50

Chapter 7: The Long Surface and The Oort Relay 61

Chapter 8: Mission to the Halo 78

Chapter 9: The Decision 94

Chapter 10: The HALO-1 Probe 99

Chapter 11: The Second Reply 103

Chapter 12: The Distortion 114

Chapter 13: The Corridor 120

Chapter 14: The Map of Nodes 128

Chapter 15: Traffic 135

Chapter 16: The Encounter 141

Chapter 17: The Adjustment 147

Chapter 18: Arrival Vector 153
Chapter 19: Node Activation 160
Chapter 20: The Synchronization 166
Chapter 21: Network Online 172
Chapter 22: The Request 179
Chapter 23: The First Reply 186
Chapter 24: Emergence 191
Chapter 25: First Contact 197
Chapter 26: The Language Between Minds 204
Chapter 27: The Chorus 212
Chapter 28: The Corridor Equation 220
Chapter 29: The Builders 227
Chapter 30: The Second Structure 239
Chapter 31: The Archive 247
Chapter 32: The First Image 255
Chapter 33: The Silence 263
Chapter 34: The Trajectory 270
Chapter 35: The Advantage 276
Chapter 36: The Observatory 282
Chapter 37: Arrival 288
Chapter 38: The First Exchange 295
Chapter 39: The Builders' Path 300
Chapter 40: The Question 307
Chapter 41: First Step 312
Chapter 42: The Long Future 316
Postscript: The Alignment Network 321
Appendix: Global Considerations 322

About the Author 325
Back Cover Copy 325
Description 326
The Seven Keys 327
More Books by Mark Anderson, PhD 328

Preface

The Alignment Echo III

The Alignment Network

Every discovery begins with a question.

Sometimes the question is simple: *What is that signal?*
Sometimes it grows larger: *What system produced it?*
And occasionally it becomes something far more profound: *What does it mean to belong to a universe filled with intelligence?*

The story of *The Alignment Echo* began with a signal — a quiet anomaly noticed in Poland, then in the outer darkness of our own solar system. What followed was not a dramatic invasion or a sudden revelation, but something slower and perhaps more realistic: a process of discovery.

Scientists observed.
Engineers investigated.
Linguists searched for patterns.
And humanity gradually realized that the universe might be organized in ways we had never imagined.

In the first book, the mystery appeared as a distant echo.

In the second, the echo revealed a hidden structure — a system that had quietly touched Earth in ways we had not yet understood.

Now the story expands outward.

Echo III explores what might happen when humanity finally reaches the edge of that system and discovers that it is part of something much larger: a network built not by a single civilization, but by many, over immense stretches of time.

The ideas behind this story draw inspiration from real scientific exploration — from deep-oceans to distant galaxies, from gravitational physics to the possibility that intelligence itself may leave structures in the universe long after individual civilizations have passed.

But at its heart, this story is not about technology.

It is about curiosity.

It is about the quiet discipline required to observe before acting, to understand before intervening, and to recognize that some of the most important discoveries in history have come not from rushing forward, but from learning when to pause.

Humanity has spent centuries looking outward into the night sky, wondering whether we are alone.

This trilogy explores a different possibility.

What if the universe has been quietly waiting for us to notice something that has always been there?

Dramatis Personae

Dr. Lin Tao
Astrophysicist, gravitational theory, and systems analyst. One of the first scientists to interpret the gravitational signals associated with the Alignment Network. Lin serves as a key scientific advisor to the Global Node Council and helps coordinate the HALO-EX-1 (aka HALO-1) mission.

Dr. Priya Ramanathan
Aerospace engineer and deep-space systems specialist. Priya leads the HALO-EX-1 probe development team and oversees mission operations as humanity begins exploring the gravitational corridor network.

Dr. Mateo Alvarez
Extreme-environment expedition leader and former deep-ocean exploration commander. Co-designer of ATHENA-MO. Mateo becomes one of the principal mission coordinators responsible for integrating scientific discovery with operational exploration.

Dr. Sanna Lehtinen
Linguist and proto-writing specialist from Finland. Sanna plays a crucial role in interpreting symbolic and structural communication from the Alignment Network and helps establish humanity's first successful linguistic exchange with another civilization.

Kai Morgan — Photojournalist & Field Documentarian
An internationally recognized photojournalist who documents major scientific expeditions and moments of discovery. Often found at the edges of historic events, quietly recording what others overlook. Morgan holds doctorates in

astrophysics, visual anthropology, and artificial intelligence, an unusual academic path that bridges the study of the cosmos, culture, and cognition. AI consultant for the ATHENA-MO. Yet he chose the camera over the laboratory, believing that understanding humanity's reaction to discovery may be as important as the discovery itself. His quiet presence and unassuming manner often allow him to observe moments others miss.

HALO-EX-1: Heliospheric Alignment Link Observatory - Exploration Probe

ATHENA-MO
Adaptive Terrestrial Heuristic Exploration and Network Analysis – Mobile Operations Unit

• **Adaptive** – The system continually learns and updates its analytical models as new observatory data, signals, and environmental inputs are decoded and integrated.

• **Terrestrial** – Serves as humanity's Earth-based analytic interface with the Alignment infrastructure, linking planetary observatories, research networks, and deep-space monitoring systems.

• **Heuristic Exploration** – Employs heuristic and probabilistic analysis to detect patterns within unknown or partially understood data, including anomalous signals, structural artifacts, and non-standard physical phenomena.

• **Network Analysis** – Analyzes the Alignment Network by mapping nodes, signal pathways, synchronization intervals, and communication architectures between participating civilizations.

• **Mobile** – ATHENA's humanoid robotic embodiment, engineered as an autonomous mobile platform capable of operating within complex, unpredictable, and dynamic environments. The system incorporates multi-axis articulated locomotion with oil-filled, pressure-balanced joint assemblies, high-precision manipulation actuators, and distributed multi-modal sensor networks integrated through onboard high-performance computational systems and real-time sensor-fusion frameworks. This architecture allows **ATHENA-MO** to navigate terrain, manipulate objects, and execute mission tasks while continuously sensing, analyzing, and responding to environmental conditions.

• **Operations** – Integrated AI-driven logistics, planning, and environmental management capabilities operating autonomously, through programmed response directives, or via a human mobile interface. This architecture enables **ATHENA-MO** to coordinate mission functions while continuously transmitting and receiving data, imagery, and operational heuristics in real-time, supporting objective analysis and minimizing potential bias or systematic error.

Prologue: The First Light

Their star was dying.
There was no longer any doubt.

The astronomers had known it for centuries, but the final confirmation arrived only months ago, when the outer atmosphere began to expand faster than any model predicted.

From orbit, the star looked swollen and unstable, its surface boiling with enormous storms of plasma.

Below it, the ocean world of Tareth rotated slowly through a sky filled with violet light.

Inside the observatory, the last scientists of their civilization gathered around the node.

The structure had taken generations to build.

Not because it was difficult.

But because they had not yet understood the universe well enough to finish it.

Until now.

The mathematician stepped forward and placed the final key into the chamber.

For a moment nothing happened.

Then the interface awakened.

Lines of light spread outward through the room, forming a map of stars across the galaxy.

One by one, faint points appeared.

Other nodes.

Other civilizations.

Some bright.

Many dark.

The mathematician watched the map and felt a quiet sense of relief.

They were not alone.

And they had never been.

He turned to the others.

“Record the message,” he said.

The transmission would take thousands of years to cross the galaxy.

But that no longer mattered.

Someone, someday, would receive it.

And the conversation would continue.

Alignment Network

Probe – Planet - Galaxy

Chapter 1: The Signal That Answered

The first signal arrived twenty-three minutes after the chamber stabilized.

No one noticed it at first.

The control room aboard the research vessel was quiet, lit only by the soft glow of instrument panels and the pale blue reflection of the ocean outside the observation windows. Above them, the night sky stretched across the Pacific like a dark mirror.

Dr. Lin Tao was still studying the chamber telemetry when the anomaly appeared.

At first it looked like noise.
A narrow spike buried in the deep-field sensor array.

The kind of thing the system filtered out automatically.

But the spike repeated.

Exactly seventeen seconds later.

And again.

Priya leaned over her shoulder.

"Instrument glitch?"

Lin didn't answer.

She adjusted the scale of the display and isolated the pattern.

The spikes weren't random.

They were separated by precise intervals.

1 pulse.
Pause.
1 pulse.
Pause.
2 pulses.
Pause.
3 pulses.

Lin felt a slow chill run down her spine.

"Mateo," she said quietly.

Dr. Mateo Alvarez, Commander, looked up from the navigation console.

"What is it?"

Lin rotated the display toward him.

"Tell me what this looks like."

Mateo studied the sequence for several seconds.

Then he frowned.

"Those intervals…"

He reached forward and typed a command, extending the time window.

The pattern continued.

Five pulses.

Eight.

Thirteen.

No one spoke.

Finally Priya whispered the word none of them wanted to say.

"Fibonacci."

"Not just Fibonacci," Lin said softly.
"The ratios are converging."

Mateo looked at the screen.

"Converging toward what?"

Lin didn't answer immediately.

Then she whispered:

"The golden ratio."

Across the room, another console chimed.

Then another.

Satellite telemetry.

Orbital magnetometers.

Deep-ocean hydrophones.

Every instrument connected to the expedition network was reporting the same thing.

The signal wasn't coming from the chamber.

It was coming from somewhere else.

Mateo slowly leaned back in his chair.

"After all this time," he murmured.

"We thought we were activating the system."

He looked at the repeating pulses crawling across the screen.

"But the system…"

He paused.

"…was answering."

In the early morning hours, the **ABYSSAL VECTOR II** began its descent.

Priya monitored the telemetry from the surface ship while the submersible crew prepared for arrival.

Nearly eleven thousand meters below, the submersible settled slowly onto the sediment floor of the trench.

Outside the thick titanium pressure sphere, the force of the ocean exceeded a thousand atmospheres. The darkness beyond the floodlights was absolute.

Lin watched the structure emerge from the gloom.

"There it is," she whispered.

The chamber stood half-buried in the seafloor — a smooth geometric form that did not belong to geology.

From the surface ship, Priya adjusted the external lighting.

"Confirming visual lock," she said.

Mateo leaned closer to the viewport.

"Still looks artificial."

Priya activated the deployment console.

"ATHENA-MO ready."

A small hatch opened beneath the submersible, releasing the **Adaptive Terrestrial Heuristic Exploration and Network Analysis Mobile Operations Unit**.

The humanoid exploration system descended slowly into the drifting silt, its armored limbs absorbing the crushing pressure with calm mechanical precision.

ATHENA's joints used **pressure-balanced, oil-filled actuators**, allowing them to function normally even under the immense weight of the ocean above.

The robot moved smoothly.

Around it, the abyssal plain stretched into darkness, a landscape shaped by millennia of falling sediment and crushing pressure.

Each step displaced small clouds of powder-fine sediment that drifted upward before settling again in the still water.

Nearly **eleven thousand meters below the surface**, the humanoid unit advanced with quiet precision across the silent seabed.

No human had ever walked here.

ATHENA would be the first.

Humanity's adaptive AI exploration system and mobile robotic interface with the Alignment Network. Analytical, tireless, and quietly observant.

Inside the submersible, Dr. Lin Tao flexed her fingers.

ATHENA mirrored the motion instantly.

The thin motion sleeves around her arms captured the movement.

On the external cameras, ATHENA's hand moved in perfect synchronization.

The system's AI corrected the motion automatically, stabilizing the robot's balance against the shifting sediment.

"The Synaptic Telepresence Model is responding perfectly," Priya said over the comms.

Mateo smiled.

"So you're walking out there without leaving your chair."

Lin nodded.

"More or less."

ATHENA stepped forward.

Its floodlights illuminated the entrance to the chamber.

"ROV floodlights now active," Priya noted over the comms.

Seven circular interfaces were embedded in the ROV unit.

Each identical.

Each waiting.

Lin took a slow breath.

For the first time, humanity had reached the structure.

Not with a diver.

Not with a probe.

But with a body built for the abyss.

"Let's see what it does," Lin said.

ATHENA reached toward the first key.

That meant someone expected this.

That eliminated coincidence.

At the back of the surface ship's control room, a photographer adjusted the lens of a small camera, documenting the events in silence.

Kai Morgan had spent most of the last decade photographing scientists at the edges of discovery.

Something about this voyage felt different from the others.

Chapter 2: The Geometry of Seven

The chamber did not look any different.

That was the unsettling part.

After everything they had experienced—the descent, the alignment of the first key, the brief pulse of light that had rippled through the ancient structure—the room had settled back into a stillness that felt indifferent to their presence.

Far below the submersible, **ATHENA stood alone inside the chamber**, its sensor array sweeping slowly across the circular console.

The seven slots were arranged around the outer ring like points on a compass, but not quite evenly spaced. At first glance they looked symmetrical, but the more the system analyzed them, the more the pattern refused to resolve into anything simple.

On the monitoring screens, Lin studied the incoming scan data.
Priya checked the streaming console and camera feeds aboard the ship.

The cramped titanium sphere of the submersible hummed quietly around them.

Mateo leaned forward in his seat beside Lin, watching the rotating reconstruction of the chamber appear in midair.

"You're seeing something," he said.

Lin didn't answer immediately. Her tablet hovered beside the display, projecting a rotating holographic model built from ATHENA's sensor mapping. She had mapped the exact positions of the seven slots and was now overlaying geometric grids across the structure.

"No," she said finally.

Mateo raised an eyebrow.

"No?"

"I'm seeing several things," Lin said. "And none of them make sense yet."

Priya's voice came through the comm system from the surface monitoring station.

"Telemetry confirms the chamber's still active," she said. "Energy readings haven't dropped since the first key was inserted."

Mateo looked toward the display where ATHENA stood motionless in the center of the ancient chamber. ATHENA quietly continued mapping.

"So it's still awake."

"More than awake," Priya replied. "The signal output has stabilized. Whatever the chamber is doing, it's running in a steady state."

Lin zoomed in on the holographic projection.

"Seven," she murmured.

Mateo looked closer.

"You keep saying that."

"Because everything about this system revolves around it."

She rotated the projection again. The chamber floor appeared in miniature above the console display: a perfect circle, the seven key slots embedded along its inner ring.

"But they're not evenly spaced," Mateo said.

Lin nodded.

"That's the strange part."

She expanded a new overlay across the model.

Lines connected the seven points.

A geometric pattern formed instantly—complex but unmistakably structured.

Mateo leaned forward.

"What am I looking at?"

Lin exhaled slowly.

"A logarithmic spiral."

Mateo frowned, one eyebrow lifting slightly.

"The same kind you see in galaxies?"

"Yes," she said.

The pattern twisted inward, each point positioned along a curve that tightened toward an invisible center.

"It's the same mathematical structure," Lin continued. "The kind that appears in hurricanes, nautilus shells, spiral galaxies—any system that grows while maintaining proportional balance."

Priya spoke again through the comm channel.

"Are you telling me the key slots are arranged like a galaxy?"

"Not like a galaxy," Lin replied.

She adjusted the model again, aligning the spiral precisely.

"They're arranged like the equation that describes a galaxy."

Mateo stared at the projection.

"Why would anyone design a door like that?"

Lin's expression darkened slightly.

"I don't think it's a door."

Priya pulled up additional telemetry feeds on the surface control console.

"If this thing is patterned after cosmic geometry," she said, "then maybe it's responding to something outside the chamber."

Lin froze.

"Outside?"

Priya began running calculations.

"Give me a moment."

Seconds passed.

The quiet hum of the chamber echoed faintly through ATHENA's audio sensors.

Then Priya spoke again, her voice suddenly sharper.

"Lin… you might want to look at this."

Mateo leaned toward the display.

"What is it?"

Priya's voice carried a mixture of excitement and disbelief.

"The chamber signal is synchronized with astronomical coordinates."

Lin blinked.

"Coordinates where?"

Priya hesitated.

"That's the part I'm trying to confirm."

More data streamed across her monitors.

Then she said the words slowly.

"There are seven targets."

Lin's tablet chimed as the new data arrived.

Seven points appeared in the holographic sky map.

Seven stars.

Seven distant locations scattered across the galaxy.

Mateo stared at the projection.

"You're saying the chamber is pointing at those?"

"Yes," Priya said.

Lin zoomed out until the entire spiral pattern of the key slots aligned with the stellar positions.

The shapes matched perfectly.

Seven points.

Seven stars.

One spiral pattern linking them all.

Lin felt a quiet chill settle across her shoulders.

"It isn't random," she whispered.

Mateo looked at her.

"What isn't?"

Lin rotated the projection again until the spiral pattern filled the cramped space between them with soft blue light.

"This system isn't measuring the keys," she said.

Mateo frowned again, one eyebrow lifting slightly.

"Then what's it measuring? Star locations?"

Lin's eyes moved slowly across the holographic sky.

Seven distant stars glowed faintly against the black.

"It's measuring us."

Priya's voice returned over the comm.

"There's something else."

Lin looked up.

"What?"

Priya's breathing had grown noticeably slower.

"Those seven stars…"

She paused.

"They're not just stars."

Lin's fingers hovered above the tablet.

"What are they?"

Priya spoke carefully.

"They're all known to host planetary systems."

Mateo let out a quiet laugh.

"Well that's comforting."

Priya ignored him.

"But that's not the strange part."

Lin's voice dropped to a whisper.

"Then what is?"

Priya took a slow, purposeful breath.

"All seven systems are estimated to be older than Earth."

Silence filled the control module.

Lin looked again at the spiral pattern.

Seven ancient star systems.

Seven positions in the sky.

Seven key slots.

Mateo rubbed the back of his neck.

"So this thing is pointing us toward seven civilizations?"

Lin shook her head slowly.

"I don't think so."

Mateo narrowed his eyes.

"Why not?"

Lin stared at the glowing spiral.

"Because if this is what I think it is…"

She swallowed.

"…then those aren't destinations."

Mateo waited.

Lin finally said the words.

"They're checkpoints."

High above the ocean, satellites tracked the chamber's signal spreading outward into space.

The transmission moved along the spiral alignment.

Across unimaginable distances.

Toward the seven ancient stars.

And for the first time in centuries—

Something on the other end responded.

That meant it was deliberate.

Chapter 3: The First Response

The response did not arrive as a signal.

At first, it arrived as silence.

Priya watched the telemetry feeds scrolling across the monitors in the surface control room. The numbers changed constantly—sensor readings from the chamber, satellite links, gravitational fluctuations, exotic particle signatures, quantum background noise, neutrino detectors, orbital observatories—but nothing dramatic appeared.

No burst.

No pulse.

No obvious message.

Just data.

But the longer she stared at the screens, the more something felt wrong.

Or perhaps not wrong.

Coordinated.

"Lin," she said quietly through the comm channel. "I need you to check something."

Below the ocean surface, Lin and Mateo watched the holographic center of the chamber. The spiral projection still glowed faintly above Lin's tablet, the seven distant star systems suspended like ghostly lanterns in the air.

"What is it?" Lin asked.

Priya hesitated.

"The neutrino detectors just logged a spike."

"The IceCube-II Neutron Observatory just relayed the spike."

Mateo narrowed his eyes.

"A spike from where? Astrophysical neutrinos are highly energetic?"

"That's the problem," Priya said.

She rotated the data window on her display, and the shared interface rotated Lin's display at the same time.

"It didn't come from Earth."

Lin studied the telemetry feed inside the cramped sphere of the submersible.

"Neutrino spike?" she said.

Above them, thousands of meters of dark water separated the submersible from the research vessel riding the surface swells.

Priya was already examining the same data.

On the ship's control deck, she rotated the data window on her display. Instantly, the holographic projection floating above Lin's computer inside the submersible rotated with it.

"The IceCube-II array in Antarctica confirmed it," Priya said over the comm channel. "Same timestamp."

Mateo studied the screen. "Neutrinos don't usually show up like that."

Kai Morgan's voice joined the channel from the surface lab. "Remind me where they normally come from."

Priya expanded the visualization.

"Mostly nuclear reactions," she said. "The Sun produces billions every second. Supernovae generate massive bursts. We also see them from neutron stars, pulsars, and gamma-ray bursts."

The display zoomed outward, showing the Milky Way.

"Some originate near active galactic nuclei—regions around supermassive black holes where particles are accelerated to extreme energies," Priya said.

She paused, then added,
"Not at the black hole itself—but within stable orbital regions surrounding it."

Mateo nodded slowly.

"Cosmic accelerators."

"Exactly," Priya said. "Places where the universe pushes particles far beyond anything we can produce on Earth."

Lin studied the spike again.

"So this one should point to something."

Priya hesitated.

"That's the strange part."

She rotated the data again, and the holographic map above Lin's console shifted in perfect synchronization.

"The trajectory doesn't line up with any known accelerator."

The cabin of the submersible went quiet except for the faint hum of the life-support systems.

Mateo leaned back slightly in his seat.

"So either we just discovered a new one…"

He looked back at the glowing spike in the data stream.

"…or something out there just noticed us."

Lin's tablet chimed.

A new dataset streamed into the blue holographic interface.

For a moment the spiral projection flickered, as though adjusting itself to new information.

Lin scanned the incoming data.

Then she stopped breathing.

Mateo noticed immediately.

"That's not good," he said.

Lin looked up slowly.

"It's not bad either."

"Then why do you look like that?"

Lin turned the tablet so he could see the display.

A line graph stretched across the screen.

Seven peaks rose from the baseline.

Seven perfectly spaced intervals.

Mateo squinted.

"That's the Fibonacci pattern again."

Lin nodded.

"Yes."

Mateo leaned closer.

"But this isn't the chamber signal."

"No."

Lin tapped the screen.

"This came from outside the solar system."

Mateo blinked.

"Outside?"

Priya's voice returned through the comm.

"I just confirmed the origin vector."

She sounded breathless.

"The signal is aligned with one of the seven stars."

Lin closed her eyes briefly.

"Which one?"

Priya answered immediately.

"The closest one in the alignment set."

Lin's fingers moved across the tablet.

A star map expanded above them.

One point glowed brighter than the others.

Mateo stared at it.

"That system is… what, a few hundred light-years away?"

"Two hundred and twelve," Priya said.

Mateo shook his head.

"That's impossible."

Lin knew why.

Any signal traveling at the speed of light from that star would take two hundred years to reach Earth.

But the chamber had activated less than an hour ago.

Mateo voiced the obvious.

"There's no way they could have answered us that fast."

Lin smiled.

"I agree."

Mateo folded his arms.

"So what are we seeing?"

Lin studied the repeating peaks in the neutrino data.

Then something occurred to her.

"Priya."

"Yes?"

"Run the timestamp comparison."

"For what?"

Lin swallowed.

"Compare the signal arrival time with the moment the chamber activated."

Priya ran the calculation.

A moment later she said quietly,

"They match."

Mateo blinked.

"Of course they match."

"No," Priya said.

"You don't understand."

Mateo felt the submersible grow colder and quieter except for the continued hum of the life-support systems.

Mateo leaned forward.
"Walk me through the assumption we're about to break."

Priya's voice had changed.

It now carried the tone of someone realizing something enormous.

"The signal didn't travel from that star."

Lin whispered,

"Then how did it arrive?"

Priya answered carefully.

"It was already here."

It had been waiting.

The chamber projection shifted again.

The spiral pattern widened.

The seven stars pulsed faintly.

Lin watched the movement unfold with a mixture of awe and dread.

Mateo noticed the change.

"What's happening now?"

Lin pointed to the projection.

"The chamber isn't transmitting."

Mateo leaned closer to the display.

"It isn't?"

"No."

Lin zoomed in on the glowing star.

The signal waveform appeared again.

Fibonacci intervals repeating endlessly.

"Those signals weren't answers."

Mateo waited.

Lin looked up at him.

"They were **acknowledgments**."

Mateo tilted his head.

"Meaning what?"

Lin took a slow, deliberate breath.

"Meaning the network already knew Earth was here."

Above the ocean, Priya watched a new stream of data flood the control systems.

Satellites relayed additional neutrino bursts.

Gravitational observatories logged faint disturbances in spacetime.

Every reading followed the same pattern.

Seven intervals.

Seven repeating peaks.

Seven responses.

Priya whispered to herself,

"Oh my God."

Deep below the waves, the chamber brightened.

For the first time since the expedition had discovered it, the ancient structure felt… alive.

Lines of light spread slowly across the circular floor.

They formed new shapes.

Not a spiral.

A map.

Mateo stared upward.

"Lin…"

She was already watching.

The chamber projection expanded outward until the entire space filled with stars.

Hundreds.

Then thousands.

Then more than they could count.

Each point of light pulsed faintly.

Some bright.

Many dark.

A few newly awakening.

Lin felt the weight of the moment settle into her chest.

"This isn't just seven stars," she whispered.

Mateo looked around the chamber hologram.

"What is it then?"

Lin stared at the expanding map.

Her voice trembled slightly.

"It's a network."

High above the Pacific, satellites relayed the chamber's signal into the global scientific grid.

Around the world, observatories began detecting the same phenomenon.

Signals arriving from across the galaxy.

Not all at once.

Not all nearby.

But enough to reveal the truth.

Humanity had not activated a machine.

Humanity had **joined a conversation**.

And the galaxy—

after millions of years of silence—

was finally answering back.

Chapter 4: The Spiral Equation

The chamber did not stop changing.

By the time Lin realized what it was doing, the chamber was already filled with light.

Not bright light.

Not blinding.

Just enough to make the ancient stone walls glow with a soft, shifting blue.

The star map continued expanding above the circular floor, its projection slowly filling the chamber like a holographic dome.

Outside the submersible, eleven kilometers of ocean pressed silently against the hull.

Mateo turned slowly, trying to take it all in.

"How many are there?"

Lin didn't answer.

She was counting.

Or trying to.

At first she thought the number might be dozens.

Then hundreds.

Then thousands.

The glowing points continued appearing across the projection until the chamber ceiling dissolved into a galaxy of faint lights.

Priya's voice broke the silence.

"I'm seeing the same thing from up here."

Her monitors displayed the chamber output in full resolution.

"What you're looking at isn't just a star map," she continued.

"It's a coordinate network."

Mateo pressed his lips together.

"Coordinate network for what?"

Priya hesitated.

"I don't know yet."

Lin zoomed out the projection.

The chamber responded instantly.

The stars shifted position until a familiar shape emerged.

A curved band of light.

Dust lanes.

A glowing central bulge.

Mateo stared.

"Is that…"

Lin nodded.

"Yes."

The projection stabilized.

It was unmistakable now.

They were looking at a model of the **Milky Way galaxy**.

Billions of stars reduced to a shimmering spiral pattern hovering above the chamber floor.

Priya exhaled slowly over the comm.

"It's mapping the galaxy."

Mateo turned toward Lin.

"But why show it to us?"

Lin didn't answer immediately.

Instead she began rotating the projection.

The seven original stars still glowed brighter than the others.

Each sat at a precise point along the galaxy's spiral arm.

Lin drew lines between them on the hologram above her computer.

The pattern appeared instantly.

A second spiral traced through the first.

Mateo leaned closer.

"That shape again."

Lin nodded.

"Yes."

The same mathematical curve appeared once more.

A logarithmic spiral.

The same pattern seen in hurricanes, shells, and galaxies.

The same pattern encoded in the chamber's seven key slots.

Mateo rubbed his temples in thought and recognition.

"So let me get this straight."

Lin waited.

"This chamber is shaped like a spiral."

"Yes."

"The seven key slots follow that spiral."

"Yes."

"And those seven stars follow it too."

"Yes."

Mateo sighed.

"That's either the biggest coincidence in the universe… or the biggest clue."

Lin smiled faintly.

"I'm going with clue."

Priya began running new simulations.

"If those seven stars are part of a larger pattern," she said, "then there might be more systems aligned along the same curve."

Her computers began analyzing the entire star map.

Millions of possible positions.

Then thousands.

Then hundreds.

Finally the simulation stabilized.

Priya leaned forward.

"You need to see this."

Lin's tablet received the update.

A new overlay appeared across the galactic map.

Additional points lit up along the spiral arm.

Not seven.

Dozens.

Mateo stared at the pattern.

"What are those?"

Priya answered quietly.

"Other nodes."

Mateo blinked.

"Additional Nodes? A pattern."

Lin zoomed closer.

Each glowing point pulsed faintly.

Not random stars.

Specific stars.

Each located along the same spiral geometry.

Lin whispered,

"Oh…"

Mateo glanced at her.

"What?"

Lin pointed to the map.

"The network isn't scattered randomly across the galaxy."

Mateo studied the pattern.

The glowing nodes followed the spiral arms perfectly.

Like lights strung along a vast cosmic highway.

Priya spoke again.

"It's organized."

Lin nodded.

"Yes."

Mateo frowned.

"But organized for what?"

Lin's mind raced.

She thought of the chamber.

The seven keys.

The signals.

The responses.

The spiral geometry connecting everything.

Then the realization arrived.

Slowly.

Inevitably.

She looked at Mateo.

"This isn't a transportation network."

Mateo tilted his head.

"No. It is much more."

Lin shook her head.

"It's a synchronization network."

Priya frowned from the surface station.

"Synchronization of what?"

Lin zoomed in on the galactic map again.

Each node pulsed faintly.

Each pulse followed the same repeating intervals.

Fibonacci spacing.

Seven beats.

Again.

And again.

And again.

Lin whispered,

"It's synchronizing civilizations."

Mateo narrowed his eyes.
"It makes sense—just not in a way we're used to."
"There are additional civilizations"

Lin gestured to the projection.

"Think about it."

She pointed to one of the distant nodes.

"If a civilization activates one of these chambers, the network knows."

Mateo nodded slowly.

"Okay…"

"And once it knows," Lin continued, "it begins communicating with the other nodes."

Priya leaned back in her chair.

"You're saying the network is… announcing us?"

Lin looked up at the glowing galaxy above them.

"Yes."

Mateo blinked.

"To who?"

Lin's answer came quietly.

"To everyone else who has reached the seven thresholds."

For several long seconds no one spoke.

The submersible hummed softly around them.

Thousands of faint lights pulsed across the spiral map.

Mateo finally broke the silence.

"How many civilizations are we talking about?"

Lin zoomed out.

The full galactic spiral filled the confined submersible.

Hundreds of faint nodes glowed along the arms.

Some bright.

Some dim.

Some dark.

Priya whispered,

"That can't be right."

Lin studied the map carefully.

Then she noticed something else.

Something that made the submersible feel suddenly colder.

"Priya…"

"Yes?"

Lin's voice dropped to nothing.

"The nodes activated, one after another, across a galaxy that had been silent for millions of years."

"Some of the nodes aren't responding."

Mateo rested his hand against his jaw.

"What does that mean? Are they nonresponsive for a reason we can understand?"

Lin zoomed in again.

Several nodes along the spiral arms remained dark.

Completely silent.

She whispered,

"I think…"

Mateo waited.

Lin finished the thought slowly.

"…those civilizations are gone."

The chamber projection shifted again.

The spiral holographic map rotated slowly.

The seven original stars pulsed brighter.

Mateo looked up.

"Now what?"

Lin stared at the center of the projection.

At the glowing heart of the galaxy.

A new point of light appeared there.

Brighter than any other node.

Much brighter.

Priya noticed it at the same moment.

"Lin…"

"Yes?"

Priya's voice had become very quiet.

"That signal isn't coming from one of the spiral arms."

Lin already knew.

She whispered,

"It's coming from the galactic center."

Mateo looked between them.

"And that means what?"

Lin felt a strange mixture of excitement and dread.

"It means…"

She swallowed.

"…something at the center of the galaxy is coordinating the network."

Chapter 5: The Central Signal

The signal from the galactic center did not behave like the others.

Priya noticed it first.

At the surface control station, her monitors were already crowded with overlapping streams of data: neutrino detections, gravitational sensor readings, deep-space telescope feeds, and the steady telemetry from the chamber far below the ocean floor.

But one pattern stood out immediately.

It was too precise.

She leaned closer to the screen.

"Lin," she said quietly into the comm channel. "I think something just changed."

Below the waves, the chamber glowed softly while Lin and Mateo watched. The holographic map of the Milky Way still filled the room, its spiral arms stretching across the curved ceiling like luminous rivers of stars.

"What changed?" Lin asked.

Priya highlighted the new signal pattern and transmitted it to Lin's tablet.

The data appeared instantly.

Lin stared at it.

Mateo watched her expression shift.

"That's different," he said.

Lin carefully reviewed the data.

"Yes."

The earlier signals had come from the seven aligned star systems. They followed the same repeating intervals—Fibonacci timing, seven-beat structure, the rhythmic acknowledgments that now defined the network.

But this signal was different.

Its pattern was longer.

More complex.

Mateo leaned towards Lin's shoulder.

Mateo studied the display for a moment longer.
"Tell me the consequence—not the observation."

Lin expanded the waveform.

The pattern stretched across the display like a staircase.

Seven pulses.

Pause.

Seven pulses again.

But the intervals between the sequences kept changing.

Increasing.

Then decreasing.

Then repeating.

Mateo tilted his head slightly.

"That looks like… I don't know."

Lin whispered,

"A coordinate transform."

Mateo blinked.

"A coordinate transform?" "Please show me."

Lin pointed to the display.

"This pattern isn't just timing. It's encoding spatial relationships."

Priya joined the analysis from the surface station.

"I see it now," she said.

The waveform rotated on their displays as the computers interpreted the signal structure.

A three-dimensional grid slowly appeared.

Mateo stared at the projection.

"Those are indeed acting as coordinates."

Lin nodded.

"Yes."

Mateo looked back at the galactic map still hovering above them.

"Coordinates to where?"

Lin adjusted the alignment.

The grid expanded outward.

Then the chamber projection shifted.

The Milky Way map rotated until the galactic center appeared directly overhead.

At the center of the projection, a single node pulsed with intense brightness.

Far brighter than the others.

Priya whispered over the comm channel,

"That signal is originating from there."

Mateo folded his arms.

"That's the center of the galaxy."

Lin nodded.

"Yes."

Priya's voice carried a note of disbelief over the comms.

"The core node is responding to us."

The galactic center was not a quiet place.

Astronomers had studied it for decades.

At its heart lay the supermassive black hole known as **Sagittarius A***.

Even light struggled to escape the gravity well surrounding the region.

Millions of stars orbited it in chaotic clusters.

Radiation storms swept through the region.

Gravity warped space itself.

It was the last place anyone would expect to find something stable.

And yet—

The brightest node in the network map pulsed precisely at that location.

Mateo shook his head.

"That can't be right, or it is not the full answer."

Lin didn't answer immediately.

She was running simulations on the signal pattern.

The coordinates were transforming again.

Expanding outward from the galactic center.

Tracing lines across the spiral arms.

Linking node to node.

Priya watched the same process unfold on her screens above the waves.

"The signal isn't just coming from the center," she said slowly.

"It's propagating through the network."

Mateo glanced up.

"Meaning?"

Lin finished the calculation.

The result appeared as a glowing web across the galactic map.

Every active node pulsed in sequence.

Like lights turning on along an enormous spiral highway.

Lin exhaled softly.

"It's synchronizing the network."

Mateo raised an eyebrow.

"Synchronizing with us and I presume with the others?"

Lin nodded.

"Yes."

Priya leaned back in her chair.

"So the moment we activated the chamber…"

She didn't finish the sentence.

Mateo did.

"The entire network woke up."

For several seconds the chamber remained silent.

Then the signal changed again.

The waveform condensed into a new structure.

Lin's tablet emitted a soft tone.

"Another pattern," she said.

Mateo looked down.

"What kind?"

Lin zoomed in.

Seven pulses.

Pause.

Seven pulses again.

But now each sequence contained subtle variations.

Small shifts in amplitude.

Minor timing differences.

Mateo tilted his head.

"That looks like…"

He hesitated.

"Like what?"

Mateo shrugged.

"Like someone trying to form words."

Lin stared at the display, trying to understand what she was seeing.

Her mind raced through possibilities.

Then she said quietly,

"If I catch your thoughts, I think we need a linguist."

That changed the timeline.

High above the Pacific, telescopes across Earth were already turning toward the galactic center.

Astronomers watched the faint pulses arriving through neutrino detectors and gravitational observatories.

Across the globe, scientists began realizing the same thing at the same moment.

The signals were not random.

They were structured.

And structure meant intention.

Far across the Milky Way, the Alignment Network had begun to speak.

Humanity simply did not yet understand the language.

Chapter 6: The Linguist

The message arrived in Helsinki just after sunrise.

Dr. Sanna Lehtinen had been awake for two hours already.

Winter light filtered softly through the tall windows of her office at the University of Helsinki, casting pale blue reflections across the piles of research papers and notebooks scattered across her desk. Outside, the harbor ice creaked quietly as the first ferries of the morning pushed through the frozen water.

Sanna had been reviewing Bronze Age symbol structures when her computer chimed.

An encrypted transmission request.

International scientific priority.

She frowned slightly. Then inhaled slowly.

Then she opened it.

The sender made her sit up.

Priya Ramanathan

Sanna smiled faintly.

"Now that," she murmured to herself, "cannot be ordinary."

She opened the file.

Several thousand kilometers away, Mateo and Lin worked quietly inside the submersible while Priya monitored the systems from the surface ship.

The chamber still glowed softly beneath the ocean floor, its projection of the Milky Way rotating slowly overhead. ATHENA continued to update the team. The pulses from the galactic center continued at steady intervals, their complex waveform repeating like a heartbeat across the network.

Priya watched the connection status indicator on her screen.

"Link established," she said.

Mateo leaned back in his chair.

"Let's hope she has good news."

Lin glanced at the waveform again.

"She'll at least tell us if this is language."

Priya activated the video channel.

The screen flickered.

Then Dr. Sanna Lehtinen appeared.

Sanna's office was quiet behind her. Bookshelves filled with linguistics texts lined the walls, along with framed photographs of ancient tablets and carved inscriptions.

She looked calm.

Amused.

"Hello, Priya," she said.

Priya smiled.

"Hello, Sanna. Sorry for the early call."

Sanna waved the concern away.

"In Finland, this is a perfectly civilized hour."

Mateo leaned toward the camera.

"Dr. Lehtinen, I'm Mateo Alvarez."

"I know who you are," Sanna said pleasantly. "The explorer who keeps finding impossible things."

Mateo replied with an acknowledging smile.

"Well… yes."

Lin stepped into view.

"Dr. Lehtinen, we believe we've encountered a structured signal originating from a network of stellar systems."

Sanna tilted her head slightly.

"A network?"

Priya transmitted the waveform data.

"Take a look."

Sanna's screen filled with the repeating signal pattern.

Seven pulses.

Pause.

Seven pulses again.

Then the extended sequence from the galactic center.

She studied it for several minutes without speaking.

Everyone waited.

Mateo and Lin felt the confines of the submersible, the deep sea was quiet except for the faint hum of the life-support systems. Priya could feel the surface ship rolling in the deep waves and sounds of the equipment in the control room.

Finally she leaned back in her chair and took a slow, deep breath.

"Interesting."

Mateo thought for a moment and took a slow deep breath.

"Interesting?"

Sanna nodded.

"Yes."

Lin asked carefully,

"Do you recognize the structure?"

Sanna nodded again.

"Very much so."

Priya leaned forward.

"What is it?"

Sanna clasped her hands thoughtfully.

"This is not a message."

Lin blinked.

"It isn't?"

"No."

Sanna tapped her screen.

"This is something far more fundamental."

Mateo and Lin waited.

Sanna smiled slightly.

"It's a grammar."

Silence filled the submersible and the ship's control room.

Mateo broke it first.

"You're saying the signal contains rules?"

Sanna nodded.

"Yes."

Lin leaned closer to the display.

"For what kind of language?"

Sanna shook her head gently.

"That is the wrong question."

Priya frowned.

"Why?"

Sanna answered quietly.

"Because this is not the grammar of a language."

She paused.

"It is the grammar of reality."

She expanded the waveform.

The sequences rearranged themselves into groups.

Seven clusters.

Each cluster contained subtle variations in the pulses.

"Primitive writing systems behave like this," Sanna explained.

Mateo looked curious.

"You mean ancient languages?"

"Yes," she said.

"Before humans invented full alphabets, early writing systems encoded relationships rather than words."

She pulled up several images on the screen.

Ancient clay tablets covered in wedge-shaped marks.

"These are examples of **Cuneiform**."

Another image appeared.

Symbols carved into stone walls.

"And these are **Egyptian Hieroglyphs**."

Lin nodded.

"They represent ideas."

"Exactly," Sanna said.

She pointed back to the waveform.

"This signal works the same way."

Mateo crossed his arms and considered her comments carefully.

"So the galaxy is sending us hieroglyphs."

Sanna smiled.

"In a sense."

She highlighted the seven repeating clusters.

“These are conceptual layers.”

Lin’s eyes widened.

“Seven.”

“Yes.”

Sanna nodded.

“The number is not arbitrary.”

Priya leaned closer to her monitor.

“What do the layers represent?”

Sanna adjusted the signal display.

The clusters rearranged themselves into a hierarchical structure.

Then she spoke slowly.

“These layers correspond to universal properties any advanced civilization must understand.”

She pointed to the first cluster.

“Fundamental forces.”

The second.

“Matter structure.”

The third.

“Energy transfer.”

The fourth.

“Space-time geometry.”

The fifth.

“Quantum behavior.”

The sixth.

“Cosmic structure.”

She paused.

Then pointed to the final cluster.

"Civilization awareness."

Mateo stared at the screen.

"You're saying the network is teaching fundamental forces, physics, quantum behavior, cosmic structure, and civilization awareness."

Sanna shook her head.

"Not exactly."

She smiled faintly.

"It is teaching **communication**."

Lin suddenly understood.

"The seven keys."

Sanna nodded.

"Yes."

"The chamber is verifying that your civilization understands these seven layers."

Mateo leaned forward.

"So if we pass the test…"

Sanna finished the sentence.

"You join the network."

Priya's computers suddenly emitted a warning tone.

"Hold on."

She checked the telemetry feeds.

The galactic center signal had changed again.

The pulse intervals were shifting.

New sequences appeared in the waveform.

Lin stared at the display, trying to understand what she was seeing.

What is that?"

Priya ran the decoding algorithm.

Then her eyes widened.

"Those aren't abstract symbols anymore."

Mateo looked up.

"What do you mean?"

Priya whispered,

"They're coordinates."

Lin looked back toward Sanna's screen.

"Coordinates to where?"

Sanna studied the new data.

For the first time since the call began, her calm expression changed.

Just slightly.

"Not where," she said quietly.

"**When.**"

Mateo looked up at the galactic map.

"You're telling us this network doesn't just connect places."

Sanna nodded slowly.

"It connects moments," she said.

Deep below the Pacific, thousands of meters of black water pressed silently against the hull as the submersible slowly released its ballast. Mateo watched the instrument panel without speaking. The depth numbers began to fall immediately.

10,874 meters.
10,500 meters.
10,000 meters.

Lin glanced at the display, and then back toward the central console where ATHENA sat secure in its containment cradle.

"Three to four hours," Mateo said quietly. "Same profile as the old trench dives."

Lin nodded. She had read the mission reports. The pioneers of deep exploration—Trieste, Limiting Factor, Deepsea Challenger—had all followed the same rhythm. A slow climb through miles of water while the world above remained completely unaware.

Lin checked the telemetry,
"Ballast release confirmed."

Outside the viewport, there was nothing but darkness.

Inside, the cabin pressure remained steady at one atmosphere. No decompression procedures. No staged ascent. The pressure sphere protected them the entire time.

Mateo leaned back slightly in his seat.

"We're already rising at about a meter per second."

The submersible continued its slow climb through the abyss.

For a long time, neither of them spoke.

Only the quiet hum of circulation fans and the occasional click of a relay broke the silence.

Above them, nearly eleven kilometers away, the Pacific surface moved under moonlight.

Below them, the trench was already fading into the darkness.

It wasn't just a signal anymore.

It was becoming something structured.

The first hint of blue appeared through the viewport.

Not bright.

Just a faint shift in the color of the water.

Lin noticed it first.

"We're approaching the photic layer."

Mateo nodded.

"About two hundred meters from the surface."

The communications panel suddenly crackled to life.

"**ABYSSAL VECTOR II, this is R/V Horizon Vector. Sonar contact confirmed at two hundred meters. Maintain ascent rate.**"

Mateo keyed the transmitter.

"**Horizon Vector, this is ABYSSAL VECTOR II. Copy sonar contact. All systems nominal. Continuing ascent.**"

A brief pause followed as the signal echoed across the water.

Then the reply came back through the speaker.

"**ABYSSAL VECTOR II, this is Horizon Vector. Roger that. Recovery deck standing by.**"

Lin glanced at the depth display as the numbers continued to fall.

180 meters.

Lin leaned closer to the viewport as the water outside gradually brightened.

Sunlight filtered down in pale columns.

Then the hull shuddered slightly as the sub broke through the surface.

The Pacific opened around them.

Moments later the support ship appeared overhead.

Massive.

Steel gray.

Waiting.

Recovery cranes rotated slowly into position as deck crew moved across the platform.

Mateo exhaled for what felt like the first time in hours.

“Home.”

Lin smiled faintly.

“Not quite.”

Above them the ship’s recovery rig lowered toward the submersible.

And somewhere far away, across the planet, Sanna was still speaking.

Chapter 7: The Long Surface and The Oort Relay

The hatch opened slowly.

Cold ocean air rushed into the pressure sphere as the locking bolts disengaged one by one. For a moment Mateo remained seated, listening to the sounds of the surface world returning around them.

Wind.

Metal cables tightening.

Voices moving across the deck.

After hours of quiet darkness in the trench, the sounds felt strangely loud.

Lin unclipped the last of the restraints from the equipment console.

"Pressure equalized," she said.

Mateo nodded and rotated the internal hatch lever.

The circular hatch swung open.

Bright daylight flooded the cabin.

A deck technician leaned over the opening.

"Welcome back," he said with a grin. "You two picked a hell of a place to go sightseeing."

Mateo climbed out first, gripping the outer ladder as the submersible gently rocked in the recovery cradle. The Pacific stretched to the horizon in every direction, sunlight reflecting off long rolling swells.

The support ship towered above the small pressure sphere, its deck crowded with equipment and recovery crews.

Lin followed a moment later.

The moment her boots touched the deck, the mission suddenly felt real again.

Hours earlier they had been nearly **eleven kilometers beneath the ocean**.

Now the world was wide and open again.

A medical officer approached immediately.

"Routine check," he said calmly. "Standard post-dive protocol."

Mateo gave a small nod.

"No decompression risk," the officer continued. "But we check for fatigue, temperature stress, and CO_2 exposure."

Lin flexed her hands slightly.

"Understood."

Behind them, the recovery team had already begun lifting the equipment container from the sub.

The reinforced transport had protected **ATHENA and it now** rose slowly from the hull cradle.

Every movement on deck suddenly became more deliberate.

More careful.

Mateo watched as ATHENA was secured onto the deck transport rig.

"That stays under controlled access," he said.

The operations supervisor nodded immediately.

"Already arranged. Restricted section of the ship."

Lin turned toward Mateo.

"How far are we from Guam?"

"About 280 nautical miles."

"At hydrofoil speed?"

Mateo did the calculation automatically.

"Three hours if we push it."

Lin raised an eyebrow.

"Someone's eager."

Mateo looked back at ATHENA.

"We lost too much time already."

The supervisor stepped closer.

"Helicopter transfer is also available."

Mateo shook his head.

"No."

The man paused.

"Any reason?"

Mateo answered calmly.

"ATHENA doesn't leave controlled security."

Lin understood immediately.

Aircraft vibration. Transport shock. Unsecured data transfer.

Too many unknowns.

Mateo continued.

"We move her by ship to Guam. From there we fly."

The supervisor nodded.

"Understood."

Across the deck ATHENA-MO locked into its reinforced transport frame with a soft metallic click.

For a moment everyone nearby paused.

The machine that had mapped the impossible chamber on the ocean floor was now sitting quietly on the deck.

Silent.

Waiting.

Lin crossed her arms and watched the Pacific horizon.

"Funny," she said.

Mateo glanced at her.

"What?"

"We just came back from the deepest place on Earth."

Mateo looked out across the water.

"And the real mystery," she added softly, "has only just started."

Far above them the sun continued its slow arc across the sky.

Behind them, thousands of meters below the ship, the trench had already swallowed their tracks.

But the signal they had discovered there was still traveling.

Still expanding.

Still waiting.

And somewhere across the planet, Sanna was already preparing the next question.

The deck of the **R/V Horizon Vector** was already settling back into its operational rhythm.

ATHENA was in controlled security and technicians connected diagnostic cables along its sensor arrays.

Mateo watched for a moment longer.

"Full vehicle integrity?" he asked.

The operations supervisor nodded.

"External frame intact. No visible structural damage. Power systems isolated."

Mateo gave a small approving nod.

"Good."

Lin glanced at the ship's horizon.

"Command center?"

Mateo nodded.

"Let's see what ATHENA actually brought back."

They crossed the deck together, stepping past rows of equipment containers and communication antennas as the wind rolled across the Pacific.

A crew member held the hatch open for them.

Inside, the ship felt completely different.

Quiet.

Controlled.

Banks of monitors filled the command room walls while satellite communication systems hummed softly overhead.

The mission controller turned as they entered.

"Dr. Alvarez. Dr. Lin."

Mateo nodded.

"Status."

"ATHENA's data core is already linked to the ship's processing system. Initial upload complete."

Lin raised an eyebrow.

"That was fast."

Priya and the technician both smiled slightly.

"ATHENA compresses mission data during ascent."

Mateo stepped closer to the central display.

"Bring it up."

The main screen flickered.

Then stabilized.

The first images from the trench appeared.

The chamber.

The impossible geometric structure carved into the abyssal rock.

For a moment no one spoke.

Lin folded her arms slowly.

“Still looks impossible.”

Mateo leaned closer.

“Play the final scan sequence.”

Priya tapped the console.

ATHENA’s sonar mapping replayed across the display.

Layer after layer of three-dimensional geometry appeared as the system reconstructed the structure they had discovered.

Then something changed.

The software paused.

A small indicator flashed in the corner of the screen.

Priya frowned.

“That’s odd.”

Mateo looked up.

“What is it?”

Priya pointed.

“ATHENA flagged an anomaly during the final scan.”

Lin stepped closer.

“Show it.”

The display zoomed automatically.

At first it looked like noise in the data.

Random interference.

Then the pattern stabilized.

A repeating sequence appeared within the sonar return.

Not part of the chamber.

Not part of the rock.

Something else.

The room fell silent.

Lin spoke first.

"That's not environmental."

Mateo didn't answer immediately.

He was watching the pattern carefully.

Priya and the technician adjusted the processing filters.

The signal clarified.

Then everyone in the room saw it.

A repeating interval.

Perfectly regular.

Mateo exhaled slowly.
"Okay… so this isn't discovery anymore."

He glanced at Lin.
"This is participation."

Lin shook her head.

"No."

She pointed to the display.

"That's intentional."

At that moment the main communication screen activated.

A familiar face appeared.

Sanna.

"Mateo," she said immediately.

"I'm seeing the data stream now."

Mateo didn't take his eyes off the display.

"Then tell me you see it too."

Mateo didn't raise his voice.

"Then we stop treating this like data," he said.
"And start treating it like intent."

Sanna looked down briefly at her console.

When she looked back up, her expression had changed.

"Yes."

She paused.

"That's a signal."

The room went completely still.

Outside the command center windows, the Pacific rolled quietly beneath the afternoon sun.

Somewhere deep inside ATHENA's memory banks, the pattern continued repeating.

Waiting to be understood.

Mateo finally spoke.

"Prepare the hydrofoil."

Lin looked at him.

"You're leaving already?"

Mateo nodded toward the display.

"If that signal is what I think it is…"

He turned back toward the screen.

"…we don't have time to waste."

The hydrofoil was already waiting.

It floated just off the starboard side of the **R/V Horizon Vector**, its narrow hull rocking lightly in the Pacific swell. Unlike the heavy research vessel behind it, the hydrofoil looked built for speed—sleek, compact, and unmistakably military.

Two extended carbon-fiber foils were visible beneath the waterline, ready to lift the craft above the waves once it accelerated.

Mateo stepped onto the lower deck platform with Lin beside him.

Behind them the massive hull of the **Horizon Vector** rose like a steel wall against the horizon.

Technicians were still working around ATHENA's secured transport frame on the main deck above.

Lin glanced back once.

"Feels strange leaving her behind."

Mateo shook his head.

"We're not leaving her behind."

He pointed toward the aft cargo module being lowered carefully toward the hydrofoil.

ATHENA's containment cradle descended slowly on reinforced cables.

The vehicle looked even larger now that it hung suspended between the two vessels.

"Transfer complete in two minutes," a crew officer called from the deck.

The hydrofoil's pilot leaned out from the cockpit.

"Once we lift, we'll be making about fifty knots."

Lin raised an eyebrow.

"Fast."

Mateo nodded.

"Fast enough."

The containment cradle settled into the hydrofoil's rear cargo mount with a heavy metallic click.

Locking clamps engaged instantly.

A technician gave a thumbs-up.

"ATHENA secure."

Mateo stepped aboard first, then helped Lin across the narrow boarding rail.

The moment both of them cleared the platform, the hydrofoil pilot spoke over the comm system.

"Departure clearance confirmed."

Mateo glanced back toward the research vessel.

The **R/V Horizon Vector** had already begun turning slowly into the wind.

High above the deck, communication antennas rotated toward orbiting satellites.

Inside that ship, ATHENA's data stream would continue processing.

Sanna's voice suddenly returned through Mateo's headset.

"I'm still analyzing the anomaly."

Mateo took his seat beside Lin.

"Anything new?"

A brief pause.

"Yes."

The hydrofoil engines started with a deep mechanical hum.

"I ran the signal through a pattern filter."

Lin leaned forward slightly.

"And?"

Sanna hesitated.

"That pattern you recovered from the chamber…"

The hydrofoil began to move.

Water churned behind the vessel as the engines pushed it forward across the Pacific.

"…it isn't random."

The craft accelerated rapidly.

Spray exploded along both sides of the hull.

Then the foils engaged.

With a sudden smooth lift the hydrofoil rose above the waves, skimming across the water at high speed.

The **Horizon Vector** quickly began shrinking behind them.

Lin gripped the seat arm slightly as the vessel stabilized.

"Okay," she said.

"What is it?"

Sanna's voice came through the headset again.

Calm.

Precise.

"It's repeating."

Mateo looked out toward the open ocean ahead.

"Repeating what?"

A few seconds passed.

Then Sanna answered.

"A timing sequence."

Lin frowned.

"For what?"

Sanna's voice lowered slightly.

"I'm not sure yet."

The hydrofoil continued racing westward across the Pacific.

But somewhere behind them, far beneath the ocean surface, the chamber remained silent once more.

And the signal they had discovered there was still repeating.

The aircraft waited alone at the far end of the runway.

Floodlights illuminated the sleek fuselage as ground crews finished the final loading procedures. The long, narrow delta wings of the **Vector Aerospace HST-1** stretched outward like a blade against the humid night air of **Guam**.

Lin slowed as they approached the aircraft.

"That's not a commercial transport."

Mateo shook his head.

"No."

The rear cargo ramp lowered smoothly as ATHENA's containment cradle rolled toward the aircraft on a reinforced transport platform.

The pilot stood at the base of the boarding ladder, helmet tucked under one arm.

"Dr. Alvarez."

Mateo nodded.

"Status?"

"Vector Aerospace HST-1 ready for departure," the pilot replied. "Cabin pressure locked to sea-level equivalent. Supersonic corridor approved."

Lin glanced toward the containment frame as technicians secured ATHENA inside the cargo bay.

The autonomous vehicle looked peaceful now, its titanium hull still bearing faint traces of deep-sea sediment from the trench.

"Direct to Europe?" she asked.

Mateo nodded.

"Destination **Geneva**."

The pilot gave a slight smile.

"One mid-air refueling over the North Pacific. If winds cooperate, we'll make Geneva in just under eight hours."

They climbed aboard.

Inside, the aircraft felt more like a compact research lab than a passenger cabin.

Three curved holographic displays activated the moment Mateo stepped into the command section. ATHENA's recovered telemetry began streaming instantly across the floating interface.

Lin leaned forward slightly.

"That's new."

"Adaptive mission interface," Mateo said. "Vector Aerospace built it for in-flight analysis."

The displays brightened.

Sanna appeared within the holographic field a moment later.

"I'm connected," she said calmly.

Mateo took his seat as the engines outside began to spool up.

"Any updates on the signal?"

Sanna looked down briefly at the data flowing across her console.

"Yes."

Lin looked at her.

"And?"

Sanna hesitated.

"The pattern you recovered from the trench…"

Outside, the aircraft began to roll slowly down the runway.

"…it's not just repeating."

The engines surged.

Acceleration pushed them back into their seats as the **Vector Aerospace HST-1** raced toward the end of the runway.

Sanna's voice continued calmly through the cabin.

"It's counting."

The aircraft lifted into the night sky.

Within minutes the Pacific Ocean was far below them, and the supersonic transport climbed rapidly toward the upper atmosphere.

Somewhere ahead of them, across half the planet, Geneva waited.

And whatever ATHENA had discovered at the bottom of the ocean was no longer confined to the trench.

The runway lights streaked past beneath them.

The **Vector Aerospace HST-1** accelerated with a smooth but relentless push as the engines transitioned from subsonic thrust to high-efficiency climb mode. The aircraft lifted cleanly into the humid night sky above **Guam**, banking gently west before turning north along its assigned corridor.

Within seconds the coastline disappeared behind them.

Lin glanced at the flight display.

"Climbing fast."

Mateo nodded. "Initial climb profile. We'll level briefly at forty thousand before the supersonic run."

Outside the window the dark Pacific stretched to the horizon. A thin band of cloud passed beneath them, illuminated faintly by moonlight.

Inside the cabin the holographic interfaces brightened as ATHENA's recovered data continued to stream through the aircraft's analysis system.

Sanna's image hovered above the central console.

"I'm receiving your telemetry without delay," she said.

Mateo leaned slightly forward.

"Good. Because the signal looked different before we left the ship."

Sanna nodded.

"It is."

The aircraft climbed through **45,000 feet**.

The pilot's voice came calmly through the cockpit intercom.

"Prepare for transonic transition."

Lin glanced toward the forward display.

A digital horizon floated in front of them, showing the aircraft climbing steadily toward the edge of the stratosphere.

"Mach point coming up," Mateo said quietly.

A few seconds later the aircraft shuddered imperceptibly.

Outside the window a faint vapor cone briefly formed around the wings as the **HST-1** crossed the sound barrier.

Then the vibration vanished.

The aircraft settled into an eerie smoothness.

The speed indicator climbed steadily.

Mach 1.3

Mach 1.7

Mach 2.1

The Pacific far below them became a dark, unmoving sheet.

They were now flying above **70,000 feet**.

Lin leaned back slightly.

"Feels like we're not even moving."

Mateo smiled faintly.

"That's the strange part about flying this high."

Behind them, secured in the cargo compartment, ATHENA remained silent inside its containment frame.

But its memory banks were still feeding data into the aircraft's analysis system.

The holographic display shifted.

The signal pattern appeared again.

A repeating waveform.

Sanna's voice grew quieter.

"I've isolated the timing sequence."

Mateo studied the display.

"And?"

She expanded the pattern across the holographic interface.

"It's accelerating."

Lin frowned.

"That wasn't happening earlier."

"No," Sanna replied.

"It started approximately six minutes ago."

Mateo glanced toward the dark horizon outside the aircraft.

"That's about when we went airborne."

Sanna nodded slowly.

"Yes."

The signal pulsed again across the display.

The interval shortened.

Then shortened again.

Lin folded her arms.

"Whatever generated that signal at the bottom of the trench…"

She paused.

"…it knows we were there."

For a moment no one spoke.

The aircraft continued racing silently across the upper atmosphere.

Then the pilot's voice returned over the intercom.

"Cruise profile achieved. Mach two point three. Estimated arrival **Geneva** in seven hours and forty minutes."

Mateo kept his eyes on the holographic display.

The signal pulsed again.

And again.

Each pulse arriving slightly faster than the last.

Sanna finally spoke.

"Mateo…"

"Yes?"

"I don't think it's just counting."

The signal pulsed again.

"It's synchronizing."

Outside the window the curvature of the Earth had begun to appear faintly against the black edge of space.

And somewhere behind them, far beneath the Pacific Ocean, the chamber they had visited remained silent once more.

But whatever intelligence had placed it there was no longer waiting.

Two hours into the flight the **Vector Aerospace HST-1** rendezvoused briefly with a tanker aircraft high above the northern Pacific.

The refueling took less than fifteen minutes.

By the time the fuel lines disconnected, the aircraft was already accelerating again toward Europe.

That changed the timeline.

Chapter 8: Mission to the Halo

Six hours later the lights of Europe appeared beneath them.

The **Vector Aerospace HST-1** descended smoothly through the upper atmosphere, its speed gradually bleeding away as the aircraft crossed into the controlled airspace surrounding **Geneva**.

Snow-covered peaks of the Alps reflected the early morning light along the horizon.

Inside the cabin the holographic displays were still active.

ATHENA's signal pattern continued pulsing steadily across the interface.

Lin stared at the data.

"It hasn't stopped."

Sanna's image flickered briefly on the display.

"No," she said quietly.

"And it's still accelerating."

The landing gear deployed with a muted mechanical hum.

Outside the window Lake Geneva came into view.

The aircraft touched down smoothly.

Mateo stood immediately.

"Let's move."

Lin looked once more at the signal display before the holographic interface powered down.

"Whatever that chamber is doing," she said, "it's not waiting for us to figure it out."

Mateo nodded.

"Which is why we're about to."

The ground crew handed Mateo and Lin a quick breakfast—steak and eggs wrapped in foil—and a thermos of strong black coffee.

After the long night above the Pacific, it tasted better than anything either of them could remember.

They had eaten on the hydrofoil during the run to Guam, but this was the first real meal either of them had touched since leaving the trench. Neither of them realized how hungry they were until the first bite.

The conference room in Geneva was already active when Mateo and Lin entered.

A holographic window stretched across the far wall, simulating a floor-to-ceiling view of the lake. Pale morning light shimmered across the projection, casting soft reflections across the otherwise sealed, windowless room.

Inside, the atmosphere was quiet—focused.

Waiting.

Multiple displays filled the surrounding walls, each rendering a different layer of ATHENA's recovered data.

Signal patterns.

Star maps.

Temporal sequences.

At the center of the room, the signal pulsed steadily.

The coordinates appeared gradually.

At first, the pattern looked chaotic.

Seven clusters of pulses from the galactic center signal shifted across the decoding model on Lin's tablet while Priya's algorithms attempted to interpret the structure that Dr. Sanna Lehtinen had identified.

Grammar.

Not a message.

A grammar.

Which meant the network was not transmitting sentences.

It was transmitting rules for constructing meaning.

Sanna's holographic image stood within the central projection—full scale, precise, indistinguishable from physical presence.

She was still in Helsinki.

"Slow the decoding cycle," she said calmly.

Priya adjusted the algorithm.

"Running at half speed."

Her holographic form appeared beside Sanna's, the two projections aligning seamlessly within the shared workspace.

Lin glanced at the display.

"I thought you were still on the Horizon Vector."

"I was," Priya said.

The faint background noise of an aircraft cabin filtered through her connection.

"I had to secure the remaining mission data before leaving the ship. There were several terabytes of raw sensor recordings that couldn't be transmitted over satellite."

Mateo folded his arms.

"So you're in transit."

Priya gave a small smile.

"Somewhere over the Atlantic."

"Holographic link from a commercial flight?" Lin asked.

"No," Priya replied. "Private. Secure."

She gestured toward the data.

"The connection is piggybacking through the mission relay network."

She paused, then added:

"I didn't want to miss this."

The signal pattern pulsed again across the screen.

Even through the holographic projection, Priya's expression shifted.

"That's definitely accelerating."

More precise.

Clusters began to reorganize.

The seven conceptual layers Sanna had identified earlier shifted into a new configuration.

Coordinates.

Lin leaned closer.

"Those vectors are spatial references."

Priya narrowed her eyes.

"But the scale keeps changing."

"That's intentional," Lin said.

Sanna smiled faintly.

"Yes."

Mateo adjusted ATHENA's processing parameters, watching the structure resolve in real-time.

"You sound pleased."

Sanna tilted her head slightly.
"You're not receiving a message," she said.

"You're being given a framework for understanding one."

"When a writing system begins, the first symbols usually describe **location**."

Mateo raised an eyebrow.

"You're telling me the galaxy is teaching us how to read a map."

"In a sense," Sanna said.

Priya's monitors recalculated the coordinate frame.

The galactic map disappeared.

A new reference grid appeared.

Smaller.

Much smaller.

Lin's eyes widened.

"That's not a galactic coordinate system anymore."

Mateo leaned forward.

"What is it?"

"Lin whispered,"

"It's heliocentric."

Priya confirmed instantly.

"Solar-system reference frame."

Mateo stared.

"Wait."

He looked from Lin to the screen.

"You're saying those coordinates aren't pointing to another star."

Lin gave him a small smile.

"Yes."

Priya finished the calculation.

The coordinates locked into place.

Far beyond Neptune.

Beyond the Kuiper Belt.

Near the distant boundary of the Sun's gravitational influence.

Lin slowly exhaled.

"The inner Oort Cloud."

The Geneva control room fell silent.

Even Sanna was momentarily surprised.

Mateo finally spoke.

"You're telling me there's a node of this network…"

He gestured vaguely toward the stars above them in the holograph.

"…inside our own solar system?"

Lin studied the coordinates again.

"They're extremely precise."

Priya brought up the astronomical chart.

The location hovered nearly halfway between the inner Oort Cloud and the outer region where long-period comets originate.

Mateo shook his head slowly.

"That region is basically empty."

Sanna spoke quietly.

"Empty regions are often the best places to hide infrastructure."

Mateo looked at the screen again.

"How long has it been there?"

Lin ran the orbital simulation.

The coordinates remained fixed relative to the Sun, not orbiting like a natural body.

Her voice dropped.

"It's stable."

Priya looked up from her holographic console.

"That's impossible."

Lin shook her head.

“No natural object could maintain that position for millions of years.”

Mateo sighed and looked at the data.

“So it’s artificial.”

Sanna nodded.

“Yes.”

Within hours of the initial discoveries, data was being transmitted to the meeting room of the **Global Node Council**.

The emergency meeting continued while key members from around the world either arrived in person or as holographic projections.

Large display walls filled with star maps and signal diagrams illuminated the conference chamber.

Representatives from the world’s major space agencies joined through secure links.

Scientists from NASA, the European Space Agency, the Japan Aerospace Exploration Agency, and Indian Space Research Organisation appeared across the screens.

At the center of the room the projection of the solar system rotated slowly.

The highlighted coordinates glowed faintly near the distant halo of the Oort Cloud.

Mateo stood near the main display.

“This location was decoded directly from the galactic center signal,” he explained.

A scientist from ESA leaned forward.

“You’re suggesting an alien relay station exists within our own solar system.”

Lin answered calmly.

“We’re not suggesting.”

She pointed to the coordinates.

"We're observing."

Sanna's hologram appeared again.

"The signal grammar indicates that this node serves as a **local relay**," she said.

Mateo glanced toward her image.

"Meaning?"

Sanna replied quietly.

"It is the nearest access point to the Alignment Network."

Priya displayed the simulation.

A faint sphere surrounded the Sun—the vast cloud of icy debris that marked the edge of the solar system.

A single point of light hovered within it.

Completely motionless.

"Estimated distance," Priya said.

"About twelve thousand astronomical units."

A NASA engineer whistled softly.

"That's nearly a quarter of the way to Alpha Centauri."

Mateo nodded.

"Which means reaching it will not be easy."

The room fell quiet again.

Finally someone asked the obvious question.

"If the relay has been there this entire time…"

He paused.

"…why did it never activate before?"

Sanna answered softly.

"Because the chamber had never been opened."

Deep below the ocean, the chamber pulsed faintly again.

The galactic map reappeared overhead.

Seven bright nodes glowed along the spiral arms.

Then a new light appeared.

Much closer.

Inside the solar system.

Lin watched it carefully via the remote deep sea camera they had installed.

The relay node pulsed once.

Then again.

The signal synchronized with the chamber.

Mateo looked up at the projection.

"It knows we've seen it now."

Lin nodded.

"Yes."

"And now it's waiting."

Mateo could feel the answer.

"For what?"

Lin whispered,

"For us to come."

Mateo nodded once as the gravity of the implications settled in.

After a short break for food and much-needed coffee, the meeting began again without ceremony.

Inside the Global Node Council chamber, the lights dimmed as the projection system activated. A three-dimensional model of the solar system reappeared and expanded slowly above the central table, planets tracing their orbits in soft arcs of light.

Mateo stood near the center of the room.

The atmosphere felt less like a conference and more like a moment of history.

Mateo thought he heard a familiar, faint click of a camera shutter.

Lin stood beside the main display, her tablet controlling the solar system projection.

"Distance from Earth to the relay node is estimated at twelve thousand astronomical units," she said calmly.

The model zoomed outward.

"That places it well inside the inner region of the Oort Cloud."

A NASA propulsion engineer shook his head slightly.

"That's nearly a quarter of the way to Alpha Centauri."
"Alpha Centauri sits about four-point-three-seven light-years away—roughly two hundred seventy-six thousand astronomical units."

"One light-day is more than 25 billion kilometers—about 16 billion miles," Priya said from the control station. "A radio signal takes 24 hours to get there. That means one light-year is about 63,241 astronomical units."

"With current propulsion systems, an unmanned probe could reach the relay in roughly twenty-five years."

Mateo folded his arms.

"That timeline isn't acceptable."

Several council members exchanged glances.

The ESA director leaned forward.

"You're suggesting a crewed mission?"

Mateo nodded.

"Yes."

The room erupted in quiet murmurs.

Sanna's image appeared on one of the displays.

She listened for a moment before speaking.

"The network signal contains an explicit spatial reference," she said.

Lin nodded.

"It does."

Sanna continued calmly.

"That means the system expects the discovering civilization to travel to the relay."

The NASA engineer frowned.

"Expecting something doesn't mean we should do it immediately."

Mateo looked toward the projection.

The relay node pulsed again.

A soft blue light at the edge of the solar system.

"We activated the chamber," he said quietly.

"Which activated the network."

He turned toward the council.

"If the network has been waiting for civilizations to reach this stage, then that relay is the next step."

Lin expanded the projection again.

The Milky Way appeared above the solar system model.

Hundreds of faint nodes glowed along the spiral arms.

"Based on the signal synchronization," she said, "the relay acts as a local access point."

A JAXA systems analyst nodded.

"So the relay is essentially a modem for the galaxy."

Priya smiled faintly. Mateo hadn't noticed when she reentered the room after the break, but she was now standing quietly at the back of the room.

"That's one way to describe it."

Lin continued.

"If we want to understand the network, the relay is the nearest structure capable of explaining how it works."

A representative from ISRO spoke next.

"What do we know about the relay itself?"

Priya pulled up the preliminary scans on her computer interface.

"Very little."

The display zoomed in on the distant coordinate.

"No natural body is visible at that location," she explained.

"But the signal behavior suggests a fixed structure."

Mateo glanced toward Lin.

"Artificial."

Lin nodded.

"Yes."

The council chair spoke for the first time.

"If this object has existed inside our solar system for millions—or possibly billions—of years…"

He paused.

"…then humanity is not the first civilization the network expected to find."

The room fell silent again.

Sanna broke the silence gently.

"That may be true."

She looked directly into the camera.

"But we are the first civilization here to understand the grammar."

Lin shifted the projection again.

The spiral arms of the galaxy appeared.

"The nodes follow spiral density waves," she explained.

"These are the regions where stars and planetary systems form most frequently."

She highlighted a glowing arm of the Milky Way.

"If you wanted to build a network that emerging civilizations would eventually encounter…"

She paused.

"…this is exactly where you would place it."

Sanna nodded.

"The network doesn't chase civilizations."

She smiled faintly.

"It waits where they are born."

The council chair looked around the chamber.

"We have three possible responses," he said.

"Observation."

The solar system model rotated slowly.

"Unmanned exploration."

The relay node pulsed again.

"Or a crewed mission."

Mateo spoke before anyone else could.

"We go."

The chair raised an eyebrow.

"That quickly?"

Mateo nodded.

"The relay has already begun communicating with the chamber."

He gestured toward the distant point of light.

"And if the signal grammar is correct…"

He glanced toward Sanna.

"…then the relay is expecting contact."

Priya's console chimed softly.

She frowned.

"Hold on."

The signal waveform appeared again.

Seven pulses.

Pause.

Seven pulses again.

But now a second sequence had appeared.

A smaller pattern embedded inside the first.

Lin leaned closer.

"What is it?"

Priya ran the decoding model.

The coordinates reappeared.

The same Oort Cloud location.

But something had changed.

The pulse interval shortened.

Lin whispered,

"The relay is adjusting."

Mateo looked up.

"Adjusting for what?"

Priya finished the calculation.

Her eyes widened slightly.

"It's compensating for Earth's orbital position."

Mateo blinked.

"Meaning?"

Priya answered quietly.

"It's tracking us."

The council chamber fell silent.

Sanna spoke softly.

"That confirms the grammar interpretation."

Lin nodded.

"Yes."

The council chair leaned forward.

"So the relay knows humanity has discovered it."

Mateo looked at the projection again.

The distant point pulsed like a quiet beacon in the darkness beyond the planets.

"Yes," he said.

"And now it's waiting."

The chair exhaled slowly.

"Very well."

He looked around the chamber.

"Begin mission planning."

The solar system projection brightened slightly as a new label appeared beside the distant node.

HALO-EX-1.

Human Alignment Link Observatory — Expedition 1

"HALO-1," Priya said. "That's what we'll call it."

Far beyond Neptune, in the silent darkness of the Oort Cloud, the relay pulsed again.

For the first time in millions of years, the network had a new participant.

And somewhere deep within the Alignment Network, a signal propagated across the spiral arms of the galaxy.

A simple acknowledgment.

A new civilization had entered the conversation.

Chapter 9: The Decision

The second Global Node Council meeting was quieter than the first.

That alone made Mateo uneasy.

The chamber had triggered a discovery unlike anything in human history. A relay node inside the solar system. A network stretching across the Milky Way. Signals structured like language.

Yet now, instead of excitement, the room carried a weight of caution.

The solar system projection rotated slowly above the central table. The distant relay pulsed faintly beyond Neptune, a quiet blue beacon in the darkness of the Oort Cloud.

Mateo stood near the edge of the display.

"So what's the hesitation?" he asked.

A representative from NASA answered.

"Distance."

He enlarged the outer solar system on the display.

"Twelve thousand astronomical units."

Lin crossed her arms.

"That didn't stop us from studying Voyager."

The engineer nodded.

"Voyager took decades."

Priya added quietly,

"And the relay is responding *now*."

A scientist from the European Space Agency leaned forward.

"The greater concern is risk."

The relay node pulsed again on the projection.

"We have no idea what that structure is capable of."

Mateo shrugged slightly.

"Neither did the first people who sailed across oceans."

The scientist did not smile.

"This is not an ocean."

Dr. Sanna Lehtinen appeared on the main display from Helsinki.

She had been quiet through most of the discussion.

Now she spoke.

"The signal grammar provides a clue."

Lin looked up.

"What kind of clue?"

Sanna enlarged the waveform.

Seven pulses.

Pause.

Seven pulses again.

"But the second sequence is different," she said.

Priya nodded.

"The structure expands when we send analysis data back to the chamber."

Sanna smiled faintly.

"Exactly."

Mateo nodded once, absorbing the gravity of the implications.

"Meaning?"

Sanna folded her hands calmly.

"The network expects analysis."

Silence spread through the room.

Lin suddenly understood.

"You're saying the relay was designed to be studied."

Sanna nodded.

"Yes."

Mateo glanced toward the distant coordinate.

"So it's waiting for someone to examine it."

"Not someone," Sanna corrected gently.

"Something."

Priya's console lit up with a new model.

A spacecraft outline appeared beside the relay coordinate.

Not large.

Not crewed.

Just a slender probe.

Mateo looked at the design.

"You've already been working on this."

Priya smiled slightly.

"Since yesterday."

Lin stepped forward.

"The probe carries a dedicated physics analysis AI."

The display zoomed into the spacecraft interior.

Sensor arrays.

Gravitational field detectors.

Quantum signal processors.

"All designed to study the relay's spacetime geometry," Lin said.

Mateo nodded slowly.

"So we send the machine first."

The ISRO representative spoke next.

"If the probe detects danger, we lose hardware."

Priya added,

"Not people."

The NASA engineer leaned back.

"That's the safest approach."

Mateo looked again at the projection.

He hated the idea of waiting years for answers.

But he also knew the council was right.

"Fine," Mateo said.

"We send the probe."

The council chair activated a new label on the display.

Heliospheric Alignment Link Observatory - Exploration Probe-One

"HALO-1," Mateo said.

Mission Objective:
Investigate the Oort Cloud Relay Node

Priya watched the signal feed closely.

The relay pulsed again.

Seven beats.

Pause.

Then the new sequence appeared.

Longer.

More complex.

Lin leaned closer.

"What changed?"

Priya replayed the waveform.

Her eyes widened slightly. "It's adjusting."

Mateo studied the screen. "For what?"

Priya answered quietly.

"For what we're about to send."

Far beyond Neptune, the relay pulsed again.

The Alignment Network had received humanity's answer.

That eliminated coincidence.

Chapter 10: The HALO-1 Probe

The world watched.

Launch had been scheduled months earlier, but the final countdown still felt unreal.

HALO-1 stood inside a massive orbital assembly dock above Earth, its slender body surrounded by the scaffolding of construction platforms and service modules.

Unlike traditional spacecraft, the probe had not been launched from the ground.

It had been built in orbit.

Component by component.

The mission had become the largest international engineering project in history.

Teams from NASA, the European Space Agency, the Japan Aerospace Exploration Agency, and the Indian Space Research Organisation, had contributed to its design.

The result floated silently against the blackness of space.

A needle-shaped probe nearly one hundred meters long.

Sensor dishes unfolded along its spine.

A wide gravitational interferometer ring surrounded its forward section.

Lin watched from mission control.

"That's our ambassador," she said softly.

Mateo stood beside her.

"Let's hope the galaxy likes it."

Priya monitored the final diagnostics.

"HALO-1 systems are green."

The probe's AI core initialized.

Billions of calculations began running simultaneously.

Spacetime modeling.

Signal grammar analysis.

Network synchronization.

The probe was not conscious.

But it could think in ways no human mind could.

Sanna watched the launch feed from Helsinki.

On her screen the signal waveform continued repeating.

Seven pulses.

Pause.

Seven pulses again.

But the pattern had begun shifting more rapidly.

She spoke quietly into the channel.

"The relay is responding."

Lin looked up.

"Already?"

"Yes."

Sanna highlighted the new sequence.

"The grammar is evolving."

Mateo hesitated, drawing a slow breath before letting it out.

"Meaning what?"

Sanna answered calmly.

"It is teaching."

The launch director's voice filled the control room.

"HALO-1 propulsion sequence starting."

Ion drives ignited first, pushing the probe slowly away from Earth's orbit.

The launch director continued:

"The ion drive doesn't shove you forward—it whispers, constantly, until you're moving faster than anything chemical could ever reach. It has already proven itself on long-duration deep-space missions."

Once the probe was clear, the main propulsion stage engaged.

The director's voice continued:

"Direct Fusion Drive, or DFD, was theoretical until recently. It doesn't allow HALO-1 to drift through space—it burns like a controlled star, pushing the ship forward with contained sunlight."

A brief pause.

"As a backup, we have a solid-fuel rocket embedded. If needed, it would require separation from the ion and fusion systems before use."

The spacecraft accelerated silently toward the outer solar system.

Lin watched the trajectory line stretch outward.

Past Mars.
Past Jupiter.
Past Saturn.
Toward the distant darkness beyond Neptune.

Mateo crossed his arms.

"First step."

Priya smiled.

"First message."

She hesitated, then added:

"We can make antimatter—but only in amounts so small they barely exist.
The problem isn't the physics. It's scale.
The moment we solve that…"

She looked toward the projection of the outer solar system.

"…we stop being a solar system species."

Far out in the Oort Cloud, the relay pulsed again.

And somewhere deep within the Alignment Network, signals began moving across the spiral arms of the galaxy.

A new node had joined the conversation.

Humanity had finally sent something to listen.

The silence of space answered—
but this time, it was listening back.

Chapter 11: The Second Reply

HALO-1 left Earth orbit quietly.

There had been no thunder of rockets, no flames reaching toward the sky. The probe had simply drifted away from the orbital construction dock and then accelerated outward, pushed by its ion engines, then by the Direct Fusion Drive, into the deep black of space.

Within days it passed the orbit of the Moon.
Within weeks it crossed Mars.

Then the long journey truly began.
That meant it was deliberate.

The control rooms on Earth never slept.

Geneva. Houston. Bangalore. Tokyo.

A continuous chain of observers tracked HALO-1's progress, their screens filled with telemetry streams, trajectory projections, and the faint, steady signal of the probe itself.

There was no sound in space—but the data told its own story.

Velocity increasing.
Power stable.
Propulsion system output nominal.

Weeks turned into months.

Beyond Mars, the Sun began to shrink—not in brightness, but in presence. It was no longer a dominating force in the sky, but a distant anchor behind the probe, a point of origin rather than a center of gravity.

HALO-1 continued to accelerate.

Slowly. Relentlessly.

A propulsion system that never stopped.

"Distance update," Priya said.

Lin glanced at the display.

"Well past the asteroid belt."

Mateo nodded.

"Still on schedule."

The projection shifted, expanding outward to show the outer planets—vast, silent markers along the probe's path.

Jupiter loomed first.

HALO-1 passed well above the giant's orbital plane, its trajectory carefully designed to avoid gravitational interference. Even at that distance, Jupiter's presence bent the surrounding space, a reminder of the scale the probe was leaving behind.

Then Saturn.

Its rings appeared only as a thin line in the visualization, delicate and precise, a fleeting elegance against the dark.

After that, the solar system opened.

No more planetary markers.
No more familiar boundaries.

Only distance.

Days later, the Direct Fusion Drive was fully engaged.

There was no visible flame—only a shift in the data.

Acceleration increased.

Not dramatically.
Not violently.
But unmistakably.

"What's the delta?" Mateo asked.

Lin checked the readout.

"Climbing. Smooth curve. No instability."

Priya allowed herself a small smile.

"Like a star learning how to breathe."

The probe surged forward—not with the brute force of chemical thrust, but with sustained, controlled power.

For the first time in human history, a spacecraft was no longer limited by the tradeoff between thrust and efficiency.

It had both.

Months passed like hours on a clock.

On Earth, governments changed.
Technologies evolved.
New missions launched and returned.

But HALO-1 accelerated outward.

Past Neptune.
Past the Kuiper Belt.

Into the vast, uncharted region beyond.

The Oort Cloud.

Priya monitored the telemetry stream scrolling across her console.

"All systems nominal," she said.

Lin nodded.

"Trajectory?"

"Perfect."

Mateo leaned back slightly.

"For now, we wait."

The relay had been waiting.

It pulsed at regular intervals, a steady beacon in the darkness. Precise. Patient. Unchanging.

Until the day HALO-1 arrived within range.

The signal from Earth took hours to reach the probe.

From the probe, it would take another twelve hours to reach the relay.

A conversation stretched across a full day of light.

Mateo stood in silence as the transmission sequence initialized.

"Send it," he said.

A narrow beam of encoded data left HALO-1, carrying with it everything humanity had chosen to say.

Mathematics.
Physics.
Language structures.
A simple declaration of presence.

We are here.

We are listening.

The room went quiet.

There was nothing more to do.

Only wait.

Twelve hours passed.

Then twenty-four.

Then thirty-six.

No one left their stations.

No one spoke unless necessary.

They all understood the moment they were living in.

For the first time, humanity had reached out—not blindly, not into silence—but toward something that had already answered once.

Priya was the first to see it.

Her voice was barely above a whisper.

“Signal… incoming.”

Lin turned sharply.

“From HALO-1?”

Priya shook her head slowly.

“No.”

She pointed to the outer system display.

“From the relay.”

The data stream appeared as a faint line at first—indistinguishable from background noise.

Then it stabilized.

Structured.

Intentional.

Different.

Mateo stepped closer to the screen.

“Decode.”

The system began parsing the signal, aligning it against known mathematical constants, searching for patterns.

Seconds passed.

Then minutes.

Then—

Lin inhaled sharply.

“It’s not just a response.”

Priya stared at the emerging structure.

“It’s a continuation.”

On the screen, the signal resolved into a sequence.

Not random.
Not repeating.

Expanding.

Building on the original transmission.

Learning from it.

Answering it.

Mateo felt something shift—something deeper than excitement, deeper than fear.

Recognition.

"We didn't just send a message," he said quietly.

"We joined a conversation."

Priya leaned closer to her screen.

"That's… strange."

Lin looked up from the data feed.

"What?"

Priya replayed the signal log.

"The relay transmission."

Mateo stepped forward.

"The seven-pulse sequence?"

"Yes," Priya said.

"But it's not coming from the relay anymore."

Silence spread across the room.

Lin stood.

"Show me."

Priya expanded the signal map.

Two locations appeared.

One marker sat in the distant Oort Cloud where the relay waited.

The second marker moved steadily outward through the solar system.

HALO-1.

Mateo blinked.

"You're saying the probe is transmitting that signal?"

Priya nodded slowly.

"But we didn't program that."

Lin studied the data carefully.

The pattern was unmistakable.

Seven pulses.

Pause.

Seven pulses again.

Exactly the same structure that had been coming from the relay node.

Mateo felt a chill.

"The probe is repeating the network signal."

Priya shook her head.

"No."

She zoomed in further.

"It's answering it."

Far beyond Jupiter's orbit, HALO-1 continued its silent flight.

Its instruments constantly measured the surrounding gravitational field.

The probe's AI analyzed the relay signal continuously, running trillions of simulations—searching for patterns.

Then something remarkable happened.

The AI solved part of the grammar.

Not the language.

The mathematics behind it.

Back on Earth, the telemetry feed changed again.

New packets appeared in the data stream.

Lin stared at them.

"These weren't in the original signal."

Priya frowned.

"You're right."

Mateo stepped closer.

"What are we looking at?"

Lin's voice dropped to a whisper.

"Equations."

The equations described something extraordinary.

Spacetime curvature models.

Gravitational field distortions.

Metric tensors shifting in patterns that none of them had seen before.

Lin's eyes widened.

"This isn't just communication."

Mateo asked quietly.

"Then what is it?"

Lin pointed to the visualization forming on the screen.

"It's instruction."

Sanna joined the call from Finland.

She looked at the equations scrolling across the display.

"The grammar structure matches the relay signal."

Lin nodded.

"The probe's AI is translating it."

Mateo folded his arms.

"So the network is teaching our probe physics."

Sanna smiled faintly.

"Yes."

She paused.

"Or testing it."

Priya replayed the signal again.

The pattern was evolving.

Seven pulses.

Pause.

Then a new sequence of geometric data.

Lin studied the shapes forming in the holographic projection.

They looked like tunnels carved through spacetime.

Curving paths through gravitational wells.

Mateo saw it too.

"Those are trajectories."

Lin shook her head slowly.

"Not exactly."

She rotated the model.

"They're corridors."

The room fell silent.

For decades physicists had speculated about manipulating spacetime itself.

Warp drives.

Wormholes.

Exotic metrics.

But the models appearing on the screen looked different.

More stable.

More elegant.

Sanna whispered the words first.

"Gravitational corridor engineering."

Far out in the darkness, HALO-1 continued its acceleration toward the relay.

But the probe was no longer just traveling.

It was learning.

And somewhere across the spiral arms of the Milky Way, the Alignment Network had begun to notice.

And across the galaxy, something ancient and vast adjusted—just slightly—to account for a new voice.

Humanity's machine had solved the first piece of the puzzle.

And the network had replied.

Humanity had received its first reply.

And it had already begun to change.

The signal wasn't just being understood.
It was being continued.

Chapter 12: The Distortion

HALO-1 had been traveling for eighty-three days when the first anomaly appeared.

The probe was far beyond the orbit of Saturn now, moving steadily outward into the darker regions of the solar system where sunlight thinned and the stars sharpened against the black.

Most of the time the spacecraft drifted through near-perfect emptiness.

Gravitational measurements remained constant.

Until they didn't.

Inside Mission Control, Priya's console flickered with a quiet alert.

At first it looked like a routine sensor correction.

Then the alert repeated.

Priya leaned forward.

"That's odd."

Lin glanced over.

"What is it?"

Priya replayed the data stream.

"HALO-1's gravitational interferometer is detecting a gradient shift."

Mateo looked at the telemetry twice.

"Meaning?"

Priya zoomed the chart.

A thin curve appeared across the display.

"Space ahead of the probe is… bending."

Lin stood up immediately.

"Show the vector map."

The holographic projection expanded into a three-dimensional model of the solar system.

HALO-1 appeared as a small point traveling outward from the Sun.

Priya overlaid the new data.

A faint distortion formed in front of the probe's path.

Not large.

Barely detectable.

But unmistakable.

Lin whispered,

"That's not normal solar gravity."

Mateo crossed his arms.

"What could cause it?"

Lin began running a quick simulation.

The computer compared HALO-1's readings with predicted gravitational models for the solar system.

Sun.
Planets.
Asteroids.

Nothing matched.

The distortion remained.

Lin stared at the result.

"This shouldn't exist."

Across the Atlantic, Dr. Sanna Lehtinen joined the call from Helsinki.

"What are you seeing?"

Priya sent the visualization from her computer at Mission Control.

Sanna watched the faint curvature ripple across the display.

Then she noticed something else.

"Is the signal still changing?"

Priya checked the waveform feed.

"Yes."

The relay pattern continued repeating.

Seven pulses.

Pause.

Then a new sequence.

Longer now.

More structured.

Sanna studied the data.

"The timing changed."

Lin froze.

"Wait."

She overlaid the signal timing with the gravitational anomaly data.

Two curves appeared.

They matched.

Exactly.

Mateo leaned closer.

"You're saying the signal and the distortion are connected?"

Lin took a slow, deep breath.

"Yes."

She pointed to the growing curve ahead of HALO-1.

"The network isn't just communicating."

She paused.

"It's shaping spacetime."

The room fell silent.

Priya adjusted the sensor filters.

The distortion became clearer.

Space itself appeared slightly compressed along a narrow path extending outward toward the distant Oort Cloud.

Mateo stared at the projection.

"That looks like a tunnel."

Lin shook her head.

"Not a tunnel."

She rotated the model.

"It's more like… a valley."

She expanded the simulation.

The gravitational curvature created a smooth gradient that gently pulled objects along its center.

No sudden forces.

No violent distortions.

Just a subtle reshaping of spacetime.

Mateo finally understood.

"You're saying the probe could fall through that."

Lin nodded.

"Yes."

Priya whispered the obvious conclusion.

"A corridor."

Back on the probe, HALO-1's instruments continued recording the anomaly.

The AI began recalculating its trajectory.

A new path appeared in its navigation system.

The probe had detected a region of spacetime where motion required **less energy**.

The AI adjusted course slightly.

HALO-1 entered the distortion.

In Mission Control, Priya saw the effect instantly.

Acceleration increased.

But the engines had not changed power.

Mateo looked at the telemetry.

"How is it speeding up?"

Lin answered quietly.

"It isn't."

She pointed to the new trajectory model.

"The distance is shrinking."

For the first time, the probe wasn't fighting distance.
It was being guided through it.

For decades, physicists had debated the possibility of manipulating spacetime.
Warp drives.
Wormholes.
Exotic matter.

But what HALO-1 was observing looked different.
Simpler.
More natural.

Sanna spoke softly from Helsinki.

"The signal wasn't a message."

Lin nodded as she studied the telemetry.
"It was instructions."
"It's not gaining speed.
The distance is collapsing."

Far ahead in the darkness, the faint relay node in the Oort Cloud pulsed again.
Seven beats.
Pause.
Seven beats again.

HALO-1 continued moving through the newly formed distortion, its path gently guided by the curvature of spacetime itself.

For the first time in human history, a spacecraft was traveling through a structure that had not existed before

—

a pathway shaped by the Alignment Network.

And the probe had just entered it.

Distances were collapsing.
Spacetime itself was being reshaped at scale.

A corridor of collapsing distance.
A four-dimensional shortcut written into spacetime itself.

Chapter 13: The Corridor

HALO-1 accelerated.

Not violently.

Not suddenly.

The telemetry showed no spike in thrust, no increase in engine output. The probe simply began covering distance faster than its propulsion system should have allowed.

Priya stared at the screen.

"That's impossible."

Lin didn't answer immediately. She was already pulling up the probe's gravitational measurements and overlaying them onto a spacetime model.

"Not impossible," she said quietly.

"Just… unfamiliar."

The holographic projection of the solar system rotated above the mission control table.

HALO-1's path appeared as a glowing line moving outward from the Sun.

Ahead of it, the distortion stretched like a narrow channel through space.

Lin magnified the region.

The curvature field became clearer.

Spacetime itself was gently sloping inward along the probe's path.

Mateo leaned closer.

"So the probe is sliding downhill."

Lin nodded.

"That's a good way to think about it."

Across the ocean, Sanna watched the simulation from her office in Helsinki.

"The signal predicted this," she said.

Priya turned.

"What do you mean?"

Sanna brought up the relay waveform again.

Seven pulses.

Pause.

Then the longer mathematical sequence that had begun appearing after HALO-1 launched.

"The structure of the signal contains geometry," she explained.

"Not language."

Lin narrowed her eyes.

"Yes."

She pointed to the equations running across the display.

"These describe spacetime curvature."

Mateo crossed his arms and leaned back.

"And the relay sent them to us."

Lin corrected him gently.

"Not exactly."

She zoomed in on the probe's telemetry.

"It sent them to HALO-1."

Priya overlaid the probe's current velocity against its engine output.

The difference was clear.

HALO-1 was traveling nearly fifteen percent faster than expected.

Without any additional thrust.

Mateo stared at the numbers.

"So the probe is moving faster because… space itself changed."

Lin nodded.

"Yes."

She rotated the simulation again.

The distortion looked less like a tunnel and more like a **channel carved through spacetime**.

Smooth.

Stable.

Elegant.

Lin began typing quickly.

Her simulation software generated a new model of the distortion.

Gravitational curvature flowed along a narrow path extending outward toward the distant Oort Cloud.

But something about the shape surprised her.

"This isn't artificial."

Priya looked up.

"What do you mean?"

Lin highlighted the edges of the corridor.

"They follow natural gravitational gradients."

Mateo frowned and raised an eyebrow.

"So the network didn't build it?"

Lin shook her head.

"No."

She leaned back in her chair.

"It **aligned it**."

Silence filled the control room.

Sanna spoke first.

"The Alignment Network."

Lin smiled faintly.

"Yes."

She pointed to the simulation.

"The network isn't forcing spacetime to bend."

"It's using places where spacetime *already wants to bend.*"

Mateo looked back at the glowing path stretching toward the outer solar system.

"Like finding a current in the ocean."

Priya nodded.

"Or a jet stream in the atmosphere."

Lin added,

"Except the current runs through spacetime."

The probe continued gliding through the corridor.

HALO-1's AI adjusted its navigation algorithms to account for the curvature.

Energy consumption dropped slightly.

Distance to the relay began decreasing faster than expected.

The model recalculated again.

Travel time had shortened.

Significantly.

Priya stared at the new estimate.

"That can't be right."

Mateo leaned over her shoulder.

"How much time did we gain?"

Priya swallowed.

"Months."

Lin looked up slowly.

"Then we need a name for this."

Mateo raised an eyebrow.

"You're naming alien physics now?"

Lin smiled.

"Only the part we understand."

She typed a new label into the simulation display.

The model updated.

GRAVITATIONAL CORRIDOR

A naturally stable spacetime channel
aligned by the network to reduce effective distance between nodes.

Sanna read the words on her screen.

"It fits the signal grammar."

Mateo nodded slowly.

"So the network builds highways between stars."

Lin shook her head.

"No."

She pointed toward the distant relay coordinate.

"It reveals them."

Far beyond the orbit of Neptune, HALO-1 continued sliding along the corridor.

The distortion grew slightly stronger as the probe moved deeper into the channel.

Ahead of it, the faint glow of the Oort Cloud relay pulsed again.

Seven beats.

Pause.

Seven beats again.

But now the pattern had changed.

A third sequence appeared.

Longer.

More complex.

Lin studied the signal carefully.

Then she whispered something that made the room fall quiet again.

"It's not just teaching the probe anymore."

Mateo looked at her.

"What is it doing?"

Lin zoomed the signal structure.

"It's preparing something."

HALO-1 continued moving through the corridor.

And somewhere far ahead, the Alignment Network was building the next step.

Within the altered spacetime surrounding the probe, light and matter remained constant.
Inside the frame of HALO-1, nothing change.

Outside, everything did.

The stars did not move aside.
They curved—
as if space itself had been folded into a long, invisible channel.

Around the probe, space and time distorted, like viewing a distant star through gravitational lensing.
Distances shrank.

Stars ahead stretched into arcs and rings.
Background space pulled inward along a narrowing path.
Light bent smoothly, not sharply.

There was no visible structure.
No walls.
No boundary.

Only a distortion—
a subtle warping, like heat rippling across asphalt.
Edges shimmered.
Objects beyond it appeared slightly displaced.

A trembling in reality,
as if space itself had lost its rigidity.

Like a groove.
A shadow carved into the fabric of the universe.

The channel did not emit light.
It redistributed it.

And the stars—
they no longer held their positions.

They flowed.

Not randomly,
but along invisible lines,
like currents in fast-moving water.

The motion revealed the structure.

Signals arrived before they were sent.
Clocks drifted, slipping quietly out of sync.
Light from ahead carried information that had not yet happened.

There was no tunnel.
No visible structure.

Only a distortion—
a softening of spacetime itself.

Light curved inward along an unseen path.
The starfield stretched, flowed—
not past the probe,
but with it.

HALO-1 was not moving through space.

"Velocity unchanged," HALO-1 reported.
"Distance decreasing."
Pause.
"Path optimal."

It was following the way space now preferred to go.

Chapter 14: The Map of Nodes

Lin realizes the corridor isn't unique. It is part of a **vast galactic lattice,** *revealing that thousands of star systems may already be connected.*

HALO-1 continued on its mission using the corridor.

From the probe's perspective nothing dramatic had changed. The stars still looked the same. The Sun had simply grown smaller behind it, shrinking into a bright point against the black.

But the telemetry told a different story.

The probe was covering distance faster than any spacecraft in history.

And it wasn't using any additional energy to do it.

Inside Mission Control, Lin studied the corridor model again.

The equations continued evolving as HALO-1 moved deeper into the distortion.

Priya watched the stream of data arriving from the probe.

"It's still updating the spacetime model."

Lin nodded.

"The corridor is dynamic."

Mateo thought for a moment.

"You mean it's changing?"

"Not randomly," Lin said.

She highlighted a new layer of the simulation.

"It's adjusting to the probe's position."

Across the world, Sanna leaned closer to her display in Helsinki.

The relay waveform had changed again.

Seven pulses.

Pause.

Then the long mathematical sequence.

But now something new appeared inside the signal structure.

A repeating geometric pattern.

Sanna's eyes widened.

"Lin."

Lin turned.

"What is it?"

Sanna enlarged the signal structure.

"This isn't just an equation."

She rotated the model.

"It's a coordinate system."

The room went quiet.

Lin overlaid the pattern onto a three-dimensional star map of the Milky Way.

At first the points looked random.

Then she adjusted the scale.

The pattern snapped into place.

Dozens of coordinates appeared across the galactic disk.

Priya stared.

"Those are star systems."

Mateo leaned forward.

"Which ones?"

Lin ran a quick cross-reference with stellar catalogues.

Names appeared beside the coordinates.

Nearby stars.

Distant stars.

Some thousands of light-years away.

Priya whispered,

"That's not a map of planets."

Lin zoomed out further.

The entire galaxy appeared on the display.

A spiral disk of hundreds of billions of stars slowly rotating around the galactic center.

Lin placed the coordinates on the galactic map.

Dots appeared along the spiral arms.

Not evenly spaced.

But unmistakably structured.

Mateo felt a chill.

"That's a network."

Priya zoomed the projection outward.

The points formed lines across the spiral arms of the galaxy.

Corridors connecting star to star.

Thousands of potential pathways.

Lin whispered,

"Oh my god."

Mateo looked at her.

"What?"

Lin rotated the galaxy model again.

The pattern became even clearer.

"The corridors follow the spiral arms."

Sanna spoke quietly.

"That would make sense."

Priya frowned.

"How?"

Sanna pulled up a model of galactic dynamics.

"Spiral arms are density waves," she explained.

"They concentrate stars and planetary systems."

Lin tilted her head and let out a slow breath.

"Which means more potential civilizations."

Mateo added,

"And more places to build relay nodes."

Lin zoomed in on several of the coordinates.

Each point sat far from its star.

Not near planets.

Not near asteroid belts.

Always in the outer boundary of the system.

Priya recognized the pattern first.

"Those distances…"

She ran another calculation.

"They're all in the same range."

Mateo tilted his head.

"What range?"

Priya answered quietly.

"Oort-cloud distances."

The realization spread slowly through the room.

Lin turned back to the galactic map.

Every node appeared near the outer gravitational halo of its star system.

The same region where the relay existed in our own solar system.

Mateo said what everyone was thinking.

"So every star system has one."

Lin shook her head.

"Not every one."

She highlighted the coordinates again.

"Only the ones that are… active."

Sanna looked back at the signal grammar.

"The network isn't just infrastructure."

Lin nodded.

"It's selective."

Mateo asked,

"Selective how?"

Sanna smiled faintly.

"It activates when a civilization becomes capable of detecting it."

Priya leaned back slowly.

"You're saying the relay didn't just appear."

Lin looked toward the distant point marking the Oort Cloud node.

"No."

She said it quietly.

"It woke up."

Far beyond Neptune, HALO-1 continued its silent journey through the gravitational corridor.

The probe's sensors kept mapping the curvature of spacetime around it.

The distortion remained stable.

As if something ahead was guiding it.

Priya checked the latest telemetry.

Then she froze.

"Lin."

Lin looked up.

"What now?"

Priya pointed to the new navigation projection.

The corridor ahead had changed again.

The curvature was growing stronger.

Much stronger.

Mateo's looked at the data.

"Is that a problem?"

Lin studied the model carefully.

Then she shook her head.

"No."

Her voice dropped slightly.

"It's something else."

The projection zoomed outward.

The corridor no longer extended only toward the relay.

It extended **beyond it**.

Much farther.

Out of the solar system.

Toward another star.

Lin whispered the realization.

"The relay isn't the destination."

Mateo asked quietly,

"Then what is?"

Lin stared at the distant end of the corridor.

"The next node."

HALO-1 was approaching the gateway to a network that stretched across the Milky Way.

And humanity had just seen the map for the first time.

Chapter 15: Traffic

HALO-1 had traveled farther from the Sun than any active spacecraft in history.

Behind it, the inner solar system had collapsed into a bright cluster of light surrounding the distant star that humanity called home.

Ahead lay the outer darkness.

The Oort Cloud.

Billions of frozen bodies drifting in slow, silent orbits.

And somewhere within that vast halo, the relay node pulsed steadily.

Seven beats.

Pause.

Seven beats again.

Inside Mission Control the telemetry wall glowed softly.

Priya monitored HALO-1's corridor navigation.

"Probe velocity still increasing," she reported.

Mateo leaned against the console.

"And the engines?"

"Same output."

Lin smiled slightly.

"Then the corridor is still holding."

HALO-1's AI continued mapping the curvature of spacetime along the path ahead.

The gravitational corridor had become clearer as the probe traveled deeper into it.

What had first appeared as a faint distortion now resembled a smooth valley carved through spacetime itself.

The probe followed the lowest slope.

Energy efficient.

Stable.

Effortless.

Then the instruments detected something new.

The alert appeared quietly in the data stream.

A subtle fluctuation in the corridor geometry.

The AI flagged it immediately.

Deviation detected.

Priya noticed the alert first.

"Lin."

Lin looked up.

"What is it?"

Priya replayed the sensor feed.

"The corridor changed."

Mateo took a short considered breath.

"Because of us?"

Lin shook her head.

"No."

She pointed to the new distortion.

"It's coming from the other direction."

The projection expanded.

HALO-1 appeared as a glowing point inside the corridor.

But farther ahead another ripple had formed.

Small.

Distant.

But unmistakable.

Mateo crossed his arms.

"That looks like motion."

Lin ran the physics model again.

The distortion was moving.

Through the corridor.

Toward the solar system.

Silence spread through the room.

Priya whispered,

"That can't be us."

Lin nodded.

"It isn't."

She enlarged the simulation.

The ripple moved steadily along the same path HALO-1 was following.

Except it was traveling the opposite direction.

Across the Atlantic, Sanna leaned closer to her monitor.

"The signal grammar changed again."

Priya checked the relay waveform.

The familiar sequence still repeated.

Seven pulses.

Pause.

Seven pulses again.

But now a new structure appeared inside the signal.

A repeating interval.

Short.

Regular.

Rhythmic.

Lin compared the timing to the moving distortion.

Her eyes widened slightly.

"They match."

Mateo looked serious.

"What matches?"

Lin rotated the model.

"The relay signal."

She pointed toward the approaching ripple.

"It's announcing something."

HALO-1's instruments recorded the distortion growing stronger.

The AI calculated its trajectory.

The moving object inside the corridor was traveling faster than the probe.

Much faster.

Estimated encounter time: 41 days.

Mateo looked at the countdown.

"So something is coming through the corridor."

Lin nodded.

"Yes."

Priya stared at the projection.

"From the other node."

The realization spread slowly through the room.

The network did not simply connect empty space.

It connected star systems.

Civilizations.

Mateo finally asked the question everyone had been avoiding.

"What if someone else is already using it?"

HALO-1 continued gliding deeper into the corridor.

The distortion ahead grew slightly stronger with each passing day.

Whatever was traveling toward the solar system remained invisible to the probe's cameras.

But the gravitational signature was unmistakable.

Something massive was moving through the corridor.

Something controlled.

Something guided.

Priya monitored the telemetry feed.

The AI had already begun calculating potential outcomes.

Possible collision.

Course adjustment.

Signal interception.

Then the system generated a new message.

External corridor traffic detected.

Mateo stared at the screen.

"Well," he said quietly.

"I guess we're not the first travelers."

Far ahead in the darkness, the relay pulsed again.

Seven beats.

Pause.

Seven beats again.

But now the pattern carried an additional sequence.

Longer.

More structured.

Welcoming.

HALO-1 continued its silent journey toward the relay.

And somewhere inside the gravitational corridor, another traveler was coming home.

Chapter 16: The Encounter

HALO-1 detected the object twenty-eight days before the projected corridor crossing.

At first it appeared only as a change in the gravitational field.

The probe's interferometers measured tiny fluctuations in spacetime curvature ahead of it—subtle ripples moving through the corridor like waves traveling along a current.

The AI analyzed the pattern.

The distortion repeated every eleven minutes.

Regular.

Deliberate.

Not natural.

Inside Mission Control, the room had been quiet for hours.

Priya was the first to speak.

"It's getting stronger."

Lin studied the sensor feed.

The moving distortion had grown significantly since the previous week.

"What's the mass estimate?"

Priya ran the calculation.

The numbers appeared on the screen.

Mateo blinked.

"That's larger than HALO-1."

"Much larger," Priya said.

The simulation expanded.

HALO-1 appeared inside the corridor, still gliding outward toward the distant relay.

The second object appeared as a bright ripple moving toward the Sun.

The closing velocity was extraordinary.

Not because either craft was accelerating.

But because the corridor itself shortened the path between them.

Lin watched the numbers update.

"Estimated encounter distance?"

Priya replied quietly.

"Two hundred thousand kilometers."

Mateo nodded slowly.

"That's practically point-blank in deep space."

Kai adjusted the camera lens but didn't take the photo immediately.

"People always expect the moment to look dramatic," he said quietly.

"It never does."

Across the Atlantic, Dr. Sanna Lehtinen watched the data from Helsinki.

"The signal grammar changed again."

Lin looked up.

"What did it do this time?"

Sanna highlighted the waveform.

Seven pulses.

Pause.

Seven pulses again.

But now a third structure had appeared.

A repeating geometric signature embedded inside the signal.

Priya compared the timing with the incoming object's motion.

"They match."

Mateo considered their inputs.

"You mean the relay is tracking it."

Lin shook her head.

"No."

She pointed at the pattern.

"It's identifying it."

HALO-1's cameras finally began resolving the object.

At first it appeared only as a faint silhouette against the stars.

Then the probe's long-range imaging system increased resolution.

The shape slowly emerged from the darkness.

Priya leaned closer to the screen.

"That's not debris."

Mateo said quietly,

"No."

The object was long.

Longer than HALO-1.

But unlike the probe's smooth structure, the approaching craft appeared segmented.

Seven large rings surrounded a central spine.

Each ring rotated slowly, producing faint distortions in the surrounding spacetime.

Lin stared at the image.

"That geometry…"

Priya whispered,

"It matches the chamber."

The rings were arranged along the craft's body at equal intervals.

Seven of them.

Each ring generating its own localized curvature field.

Together they aligned perfectly with the gravitational corridor.

Mateo crossed his arms.

"So the craft isn't fighting the corridor."

Lin nodded.

"It's tuned to it."

HALO-1's AI analyzed the craft's trajectory.

The object was not slowing down.

It remained perfectly centered inside the corridor's curvature.

As if the path had been built for it.

Priya checked the estimated age of the corridor disturbance trailing behind the craft.

Then she froze.

"Lin."

Lin looked over.

"What?"

Priya rotated the model.

"The distortion behind it…"

Her voice dropped.

"It's been traveling for centuries."

Silence spread across the control room.

Mateo finally spoke.

"So whatever that is…"

He looked back at the approaching structure.

"…it's been using the network long before we discovered it."

HALO-1 continued gliding deeper into the corridor.

The approaching craft grew clearer with each passing hour.

The seven rings glowed faintly as they interacted with the corridor's curvature.

The structure looked ancient.

Not damaged.

Not drifting.

Purposeful.

Controlled.

Sanna studied the signal pattern again.

Then she noticed something else.

"The relay just transmitted a new sequence."

Priya checked the feed.

It was different from anything they had seen before.

Longer.

Structured.

Like punctuation.

Lin translated the geometry into the signal grammar model.

Then she looked up slowly.

Mateo asked,

"What does it say?"

Lin answered quietly.

"It's announcing an arrival."

HALO-1 and the unknown craft continued moving toward each other inside the gravitational corridor.

For the first time in human history, two travelers from different civilizations were about to pass in deep space.

Not in a distant galaxy.

Not around another star.

But here.

Inside our own solar system.

Chapter 17: The Adjustment

HALO-1 continued moving through the gravitational corridor.

The probe's instruments tracked the approaching craft with increasing precision as the distance between them shrank.

Two hundred thousand kilometers.

One hundred eighty thousand.

One hundred sixty thousand.

Inside Mission Control, every scientist in the room watched the telemetry wall.

No one spoke.

Priya monitored the closing trajectory.

"Relative velocity still stable," she said quietly.

Lin nodded.

"The corridor is doing most of the work."

Mateo folded his arms.

"And the other craft?"

Priya zoomed the projection.

The object's seven rings rotated slowly, each one maintaining a stable curvature field that aligned perfectly with the corridor.

"It hasn't changed course," she said.

"Not yet."

HALO-1's cameras resolved the structure more clearly now.

The craft's central spine appeared metallic, though not reflective like modern spacecraft. The surface looked darker—ceramic.

Along the spine the seven rings were spaced evenly.

Each ring rotated with slow precision, producing a faint ripple in spacetime around the craft.

Lin studied the measurements.

"Those rings are stabilizing the corridor."

Mateo raised an eyebrow.

"So it's not just riding the corridor."

"No," Lin said.

"It's helping maintain it."

Distance to encounter: 140,000 kilometers.

Priya leaned forward.

"Telemetry update."

Lin glanced over.

"What changed?"

Priya replayed the navigation model.

HALO-1's path remained exactly the same.

But the incoming craft had shifted slightly.

Only a fraction of a degree.

Barely noticeable.

Mateo straightened for a moment.

"That looks like a course correction."

Lin recalculated the trajectories.

The result appeared immediately.

"They adjusted."

Priya turned.

"You're sure?"

Lin pointed to the model.

"If they hadn't changed course, the two objects would have passed within twenty thousand kilometers."

Mateo nodded slowly.

"And now?"

Priya checked the new estimate.

"Seventy thousand."

The control room fell silent.

Mateo said what everyone was thinking.

"They saw us."

Lin nodded.

"Yes."

Across the ocean, Sanna leaned closer to her display.

"The relay signal changed again."

Priya opened the waveform.

Seven pulses.

Pause.

Seven pulses again.

But now a new interval appeared between sequences.

Short.

Measured.

Repeating.

Lin compared it with the incoming craft's trajectory adjustment.

Her eyes widened.

"They're synchronized."

Mateo looked up.

"You mean the relay is coordinating traffic."

Lin nodded.

"Yes."

HALO-1's AI continued tracking the craft's movement.

The probe transmitted new images to Earth every few minutes.

The structure looked ancient.

The surfaces showed subtle wear, as if the craft had traveled through countless corridors over centuries.

Yet its motion remained precise.

Deliberate.

Controlled.

Distance to encounter: 90,000 kilometers.

Priya spoke quietly.

"It's rotating."

Lin looked up.

The incoming craft had turned slightly along its axis.

Not enough to change its course.

Just enough to align one of the rings toward HALO-1.

Mateo looked at the monitor to quickly confirm the data.

"It makes sense—that doesn't look like navigation."

Lin studied the new telemetry.

“No.”

She pointed to the signal feed.

“It’s communicating.”

The ring emitted a brief burst of gravitational distortion.

HALO-1’s sensors recorded the ripple as it passed through the corridor.

The waveform appeared instantly on the screens in Mission Control.

Priya stared.

“That pattern…”

Sanna spoke from Helsinki.

“It matches the network grammar.”

Lin translated the signal into the mathematical structure they had been studying for weeks.

The pattern was simple.

Short.

Clear.

Mateo looked at the translation.

“What does it mean?”

Lin hesitated.

Then she answered.

“It’s an acknowledgment.”

HALO-1 continued its silent glide through the corridor.

The unknown craft passed ahead of it, moving toward the inner solar system.

Two travelers in the same cosmic pathway.

One ancient.

One newly arrived.

For a moment they shared the same corridor in spacetime.

Then the distance between them began to grow again.

Priya watched the telemetry slowly stabilize.

"They're gone."

Mateo exhaled slowly.

"So we just had our first contact."

Lin shook her head gently.

"Not contact."

She looked toward the distant relay coordinate glowing on the projection.

"Recognition."

Far beyond Neptune, the relay pulsed again.

Seven beats.

Pause.

Seven beats again.

And somewhere deeper in the Alignment Network, a new signal spread across the spiral arms of the galaxy.

A message that had not been sent from this star system in billions of years.

A new civilization had entered the corridor.

Chapter 18: Arrival Vector

HALO-1 continued outward.

The corridor ahead remained smooth and stable, its curvature guiding the probe deeper toward the distant relay node in the outer halo of the solar system.

Behind it, the ancient craft was disappearing into the inner darkness.

For several minutes no one in Mission Control spoke.

The encounter had been brief.

Silent.

Polite.

That meant it was deliberate.

Priya finally broke the silence.

"I'm recalculating its trajectory."

Lin nodded.

"Good."

Mateo leaned over the console.

"Heading for Earth?"

Priya didn't answer immediately.

She ran the orbital projection again.

The result appeared on the main display.

The solar system expanded across the holographic map.

The incoming craft's path appeared as a curved line moving inward along the corridor.

The line passed Neptune.

Then Uranus.

Then Saturn.

Priya swallowed.

"It's not slowing down."

Lin studied the model carefully.

"Corridor dynamics are still holding."

Mateo looked excited.

"So it's riding the same pathway HALO-1 used."

"Yes," Lin said.

"But in reverse."

Across the Atlantic, Sanna watched the signal feed from Helsinki.

"The relay node just transmitted again."

Priya checked the waveform.

The familiar structure repeated.

Seven pulses.

Pause.

Seven pulses again.

But now the third sequence had grown longer.

More detailed.

Layered.

Lin translated the new signal into the mathematical structure they had been building.

Coordinates appeared inside the model.

Not galactic ones this time.

Local ones.

Solar system coordinates.

Mateo leaned forward.

"That looks like navigation."

Lin's eyes widened.

"It is."

She pointed to the inner endpoint.

The coordinates matched a location in the distant outer halo of the solar system.

Exactly where the relay node had first been detected.

Priya whispered the obvious conclusion.

"It's heading for the relay."

The room remained quiet as the implication settled in.

The craft had not been exploring.

It had been traveling along the corridor toward the solar system long before HALO-1 launched.

Their probe had simply crossed its path.

Mateo folded his arms.

"So we didn't trigger anything."

Lin shook her head.

"No."

She looked again at the incoming trajectory.

"We just happened to meet it."

HALO-1 transmitted another image of the departing craft.

The seven rotating rings glowed faintly inside the corridor's curvature.

The structure looked ancient.

Older than any human spacecraft.

Older, perhaps, than human civilization itself.

Priya examined the telemetry again.

"Energy signature is stable."

Mateo nodded.

"So it's operational."

"Yes."

Priya paused.

"Very operational."

Lin zoomed the model outward again.

The corridor stretching through the solar system looked like a luminous thread.

HALO-1 moved along one end of it.

The incoming craft moved along the other.

Both heading toward the same destination.

The relay.

Sanna spoke quietly.

"The signal grammar changed again."

Lin looked up.

"What now?"

Sanna displayed the new waveform.

Seven pulses.

Pause.

Seven pulses again.

Then a longer mathematical sequence.

Finally, a short closing structure.

Lin translated the pattern.

The words appeared slowly in the model.

Mateo stared at them.

"You're kidding."

Lin shook her head.

"No."

The translation was simple.

Not complex mathematics.

Not corridor geometry.

Just a statement embedded inside the signal grammar.

NODE APPROACH

TRAFFIC ACKNOWLEDGED

Priya leaned back slowly.

"So the network manages arrivals."

Mateo nodded.

"Like air traffic control."

Lin looked again at the trajectory lines.

"Yes."

She said it quietly.

"Except the airport is our solar system."

Far beyond Neptune, the relay pulsed again.

Seven beats.

Pause.

Seven beats again.

The ancient craft continued descending through the gravitational corridor toward the relay node.

And for the first time since humanity discovered the Alignment Network, the scientists in Mission Control understood something profound.

The solar system had not just joined the network.

It had been scheduled.

HALO-1 continued outward.

The probe was now only months from the relay.

But the incoming traveler would arrive first.

Priya checked the updated projections.

Her voice dropped slightly.

"Estimated arrival at relay node…"

Mateo waited.

"How long?"

Priya finished the calculation.

"Seventeen days."

The room went silent again.

Humanity had just discovered the Alignment Network.

And in less than three weeks, something that had been traveling the corridors for centuries would arrive at the gateway in our own solar system.

That eliminated coincidence.

That changed the timeline.

Chapter 19: Node Activation

Seventeen days passed quickly.

Too quickly.

Inside Mission Control the scientists barely left their consoles. Every hour HALO-1 transmitted new data from the gravitational corridor, and every hour the relay node in the outer solar system pulsed with slightly stronger signals.

Something was changing.

Something was waking up.

Priya noticed the first clear sign.

"Signal amplitude just doubled."

Lin looked up immediately.

"From the relay?"

Priya nodded.

"Yes."

She magnified the waveform.

Seven pulses.

Pause.

Seven pulses again.

But now each pulse carried a stronger gravitational signature.

Mateo leaned closer to the display.

"That looks like power ramping up."

Lin overlaid the new readings with HALO-1's gravitational sensors.

The corridor around the probe remained stable.

But farther ahead, near the relay node, spacetime curvature was increasing.

Gradually.

Smoothly.

As if a massive system were coming online.

Across the Atlantic, Sanna watched the signal structure evolve.

"The grammar changed again."

Lin turned.

"What does it show?"

Sanna enlarged the pattern.

"Additional layers."

Priya frowned.

"What kind of layers?"

Sanna rotated the visualization.

The signal contained several repeating structures arranged around the familiar seven-pulse pattern.

Seven clusters.

Seven geometric fields.

Lin felt a sudden realization forming.

"Wait."

She overlaid the signal geometry with the images HALO-1 had captured of the ancient craft.

Seven rotating rings.

Seven gravitational fields.

Mateo saw it too.

"They match."

The room grew very quiet.

Lin pointed to the relay node on the solar system map.

"The relay is preparing seven alignment points."

Priya whispered,

"Like docking ports."

HALO-1 transmitted a new image.

The relay node was now visible in the probe's long-range cameras as a faint structure embedded among distant icy bodies.

At first the relay had appeared invisible.

Now it glowed faintly against the darkness.

Seven arcs of energy surrounded the central structure.

Slowly rotating.

Matching the geometry of the ancient craft.

Mateo studied the projection.

"That thing is huge."

Lin nodded.

"Yes."

She zoomed the image.

The relay structure extended hundreds of kilometers across, its central body surrounded by enormous ring-like segments.

Each segment emitted faint distortions in spacetime.

Priya whispered,

"It's a corridor stabilizer."

The simulation expanded.

Seven curved fields appeared around the relay node.

Each field aligned perfectly with one of the incoming craft's rings.

The corridor geometry connected them like pieces of a puzzle.

Lin exhaled slowly.

"The craft isn't just arriving."

Mateo looked at her.

"What do you mean?"

Lin pointed to the alignment fields.

"It's docking."

Across the world, Sanna translated the newest signal layer.

Her voice remained calm, but the words carried weight.

"The grammar confirms it."

Priya looked up.

"What does it say?"

Sanna paused briefly before answering.

NODE PREPARATION

CORRIDOR ALIGNMENT

ARRIVAL SEQUENCE INITIATED

Inside Mission Control the screens glowed quietly.

Humanity had just discovered the Alignment Network.

Now they were about to witness how it worked.

In real-time.

The ancient craft continued its silent descent through the gravitational corridor.

The seven rings around its body rotated slowly as it approached the relay.

Each ring produced a localized distortion in spacetime that synchronized with the relay's growing fields.

Like two complex machines preparing to connect.

Priya checked the latest distance estimate.

"Time to node approach: nine days."

Mateo folded his arms.

"So we're about to watch an alien spacecraft dock with an alien gateway."

Lin nodded.

"Yes."

She said it quietly.

"And we're the only witnesses."

Far beyond Neptune, the relay pulsed again.

Seven beats.

Pause.

Seven beats again.

But now the pulses carried far more energy than before.

The node was no longer sleeping.

The gateway in our solar system was coming fully online.

HALO-1 continued gliding through the corridor toward the relay.

The probe's cameras recorded everything.

Every shift in spacetime.

Every change in the alignment fields.

Every movement of the ancient craft.

And for the first time since humanity discovered the Alignment Network, the scientists realized something extraordinary.

The relay was not just a communication device.

It was a **transport hub**.

A gateway connecting the corridors between stars.

The arrival sequence had begun.

Chapter 20: The Synchronization

Nine days later the relay began to glow.

At first the change was subtle.

HALO-1's cameras recorded a faint increase in luminosity around the distant structure as the alignment fields intensified. The relay node, once invisible against the dark background of the Oort Cloud, now appeared as a dim geometric silhouette surrounded by curved arcs of light.

Priya watched the feed carefully.

"It's definitely active now."

Lin nodded.

"All seven fields."

The projection in Mission Control expanded.

Seven curved alignment arcs surrounded the relay like petals of an enormous mechanical flower. Each arc produced a stable distortion in spacetime, forming the endpoints of the gravitational corridor.

Mateo leaned closer to the display.

"That looks deliberate."

Lin zoomed the model.

"It is."

She highlighted the incoming craft.

Seven rotating rings.

Each one matched perfectly with one of the relay's alignment arcs.

HALO-1 transmitted another image.

The ancient craft was now clearly visible.

The seven rings rotated slowly around its long central spine, emitting faint ripples in spacetime. Those ripples aligned exactly with the relay's growing fields.

Priya whispered,

"They're synchronizing."

Across the Atlantic, Sanna watched the relay signal.

"The grammar changed again."

Lin glanced at the waveform.

The familiar pattern remained:

Seven pulses.

Pause.

Seven pulses again.

But the structure had expanded dramatically.

Seven clusters.

Seven intervals.

Seven repeating layers.

Mateo crossed his arms.

"So the seven keys weren't symbolic."

Lin shook her head.

"No."

She said it quietly.

"They're structural."

HALO-1's sensors recorded the corridor geometry shifting as the craft approached the relay.

The distortion grew stronger.

More precise.

The corridor now resembled a narrow channel carved cleanly through spacetime.

Priya studied the telemetry.

"The alignment fields are stabilizing the corridor."

Lin nodded.

"Yes."

She pointed toward the relay.

"And the craft is completing the circuit."

Distance to relay: 600,000 kilometers.

The incoming craft slowed slightly.

Not through thrust.

Through subtle adjustments in the curvature fields generated by its rings.

The gravitational corridor itself began compressing around the relay node.

Mateo watched the simulation update.

"That's incredible."

Lin smiled faintly.

"They're locking the geometry."

HALO-1's cameras captured the moment the first ring aligned.

The relay's outer arc brightened suddenly.

Spacetime around the node rippled outward like waves across water.

Then the second ring aligned.

Another arc ignited.

Then the third.

Fourth.

Fifth.

Sixth.

Inside Mission Control no one spoke.

Seven rings.

Seven arcs.

Seven gravitational fields.

Perfectly synchronized.

The final ring rotated into position.

The moment it aligned, HALO-1's sensors recorded the largest spacetime distortion yet detected.

The relay node pulsed with enormous energy.

The corridor widened.

Stabilized.

Deepened.

Priya stared at the telemetry.

"That's not just a docking maneuver."

Lin shook her head quickly.

"No."

She pointed to the far end of the corridor projection.

The path no longer ended at the relay.

It extended outward.

Far beyond the solar system.

Far beyond the local stars.

Mateo whispered the realization.

“The gateway opened.”

HALO-1’s instruments detected a massive flow of gravitational energy stabilizing the corridor between nodes.

For the first time, the full pathway of the Alignment Network became visible.

A bridge through spacetime stretching from the relay in our solar system to another star system thousands of light-years away.

Across the ocean, Sanna translated the newest signal layer.

Her voice was quiet but steady.

“The grammar is clear.”

Priya looked up.

“What does it say?”

Sanna read the structure slowly.

CORRIDOR STABILIZED

NODE CONNECTED

TRANSIT READY

Inside Mission Control the room remained silent.

Humanity had just witnessed the activation of a galactic transportation system.

A network that had likely existed for longer than human civilization.

Perhaps longer than humanity itself.

HALO-1 continued recording everything.

Every change in spacetime.

Every fluctuation in the corridor.

Every movement of the ancient craft now docked with the relay.

And as the corridor stabilized, something unexpected appeared at the far end of the projection.

A faint ripple.

Moving toward the solar system.

Priya leaned forward slowly.

"Lin…"

Lin looked up.

"What is it?"

Priya pointed to the far end of the corridor.

Another gravitational disturbance was forming.

Mateo said the words quietly.

"Something else is coming."

Chapter 21: Network Online

For several minutes after the corridor stabilized, no one in Mission Control spoke.

HALO-1's instruments continued recording the relay node as its alignment fields maintained the corridor connection. The seven arcs surrounding the structure glowed steadily now, each one producing a precise curvature in spacetime that extended outward along the corridor.

The system looked stable.

Perfectly stable.

Priya studied the telemetry.

"All alignment fields holding."

Lin nodded.

"Corridor geometry hasn't changed."

Mateo crossed his arms.

"So the gateway is just… open."

"Yes," Lin said quietly.

"That's exactly what it is."

HALO-1 transmitted a wider image of the relay.

The ancient craft remained docked at the node, its seven rings synchronized with the relay's alignment arcs. Together they formed a larger structure—two systems working in harmony to maintain the corridor.

Priya zoomed the view.

"It's not doing anything."

Lin shook her head.

"It doesn't have to."

She pointed to the corridor projection.

"The node is now part of the network again."

Across the Atlantic, Sanna monitored the signal grammar.

"The relay signal has expanded."

Priya checked the waveform feed.

The familiar sequence still repeated.

Seven pulses.

Pause.

Seven pulses again.

But now the pattern was layered with dozens of smaller transmissions moving across the corridor channel.

Lin frowned.

"That's new."

Sanna rotated the signal structure.

"These aren't instructions."

Mateo looked up.

"What are they?"

Sanna smiled slightly.

"They're announcements."

Lin compared the signals with the galactic node map they had reconstructed earlier.

Points across the spiral arms began appearing again on the projection.

One by one.

Distant star systems.

Active nodes.

Each signal carried a small block of information.

Coordinates.

Transit status.

Corridor availability.

Priya leaned forward.

"That's network traffic."

Lin's breath caught.

"Yes."

Mateo raised an eyebrow.

"You're telling me we're listening to the galaxy's highway system."

Lin gave a small smile.

"That's a good way to describe it."

HALO-1 continued recording the corridor's structure.

The probe's sensors detected faint gravitational disturbances moving through the far end of the network.

Not objects.

Not ships.

Just the signatures of distant corridors activating and deactivating.

Mateo watched the simulation update.

"So the network is busy."

Lin nodded.

"Very busy."

Sanna examined one of the signal clusters more carefully.

"This one is closer."

Priya zoomed the map.

The coordinate appeared roughly three thousand light-years away along the Orion arm of the galaxy.

Another node.

Another corridor connection.

Mateo leaned forward.

"What are they saying about us?"

Lin translated the signal grammar.

The message structure was simple.

Short.

Formal.

She read it aloud.

NEW NODE DETECTED

SOL SYSTEM

NETWORK STATUS: ACTIVE

The room remained quiet.

Priya leaned back slowly.

"So the galaxy knows we're here now."

Lin nodded.

"Yes."

Mateo folded his arms.

"Well."

He glanced toward the glowing relay node on the projection.

"That didn't take long."

HALO-1 transmitted another update.

The probe was now less than two million kilometers from the relay.

Its cameras captured the ancient craft still docked to the node, its rings rotating slowly as the corridor remained stable.

The structure looked patient.

Waiting.

Priya checked the probe's navigation model.

"HALO-1 arrival at relay: ninety-two days."

Mateo nodded.

"So our probe will reach the node after the visitor."

"Yes," Lin said.

"And then we finally get a close look."

Across the ocean, Sanna watched the signal stream continue expanding.

More nodes appeared.

More transmissions.

The Alignment Network had fully awakened.

For the first time in billions of years, a new star system had joined it.

Far beyond Neptune, the relay pulsed again.

Seven beats.

Pause.

Seven beats again.

The gravitational corridor stretched across the darkness between stars.

And now it carried traffic.

HALO-1 continued gliding outward.

Recording everything.

Learning everything.

Serving as humanity's eyes inside the network.

Then Priya noticed something unexpected.

She leaned closer to the console.

"Lin."

Lin turned.

"What is it?"

Priya pointed to a new signal arriving through the corridor.

It was stronger than the others.

Direct.

Addressed to the relay node in the solar system.

Lin translated the structure.

The message appeared slowly on the screen.

Mateo read it aloud.

REQUEST: NODE ACCESS

ORIGIN: UNKNOWN

The room fell silent again.

The network had reopened.

And something else in the galaxy had just asked permission to come here.

Chapter 22: The Request

The message remained on the screen for a long time.

No one spoke.

Inside Mission Control the words glowed quietly against the dark background of the corridor map.

REQUEST: NODE ACCESS

ORIGIN: UNKNOWN

Priya was the first to move.

She replayed the transmission again.

"It's definitely routed through the relay."

Lin nodded.

"Yes."

She rotated the signal model.

"And the grammar matches the network structure perfectly."

Mateo took a slow, meaningful breath.

"So this is normal traffic."

"Yes," Lin said.

"For the network."

Across the ocean, Sanna leaned closer to her monitor in Helsinki.

"The message format is very simple."

Priya looked up.

"What does that mean?"

Sanna highlighted the structure.

"It's procedural."

Mateo crossed his arms.

"Like a handshake."

Lin expanded the relay model again.

The ancient craft remained docked with the node, its seven rings rotating slowly as the corridor stayed stabilized.

The system looked calm.

Patient.

As if waiting for something.

Priya checked the relay's response channel.

"It hasn't answered yet."

Lin nodded.

"That makes sense."

Mateo looked at her.

"Why?"

Lin pointed to the network grammar.

"The request isn't directed to the relay."

She paused.

"It's directed to the **node authority**."

The room went quiet.

Mateo slowly realized what she meant.

"You're saying…"

Lin finished the thought.

"That's us."

Silence filled the control room.

Humanity had spent the last months studying the Alignment Network, trying to understand how it worked.

Now the network was waiting for them to participate.

Priya leaned back.

"That seems… premature."

Lin gave a small smile.

"Yes."

Mateo nodded.

"I'd say that's an understatement."

Across the world, additional scientists joined the discussion.

Representatives from

- NASA
- European Space Agency
- Japan Aerospace Exploration Agency
- Indian Space Research Organisation

appeared on the secure conference channel.

Within minutes the meeting had become the most important conversation in human history.

Mateo listened quietly as the discussion unfolded.

Some scientists argued for caution.

Others pointed out that the network had likely operated for millions of years without catastrophic consequences.

Lin remained calm.

"The corridor already exists."

She pointed to the projection.

"If the network wanted access to our system, it could simply open the path."

Priya nodded slowly.

"So the request isn't about permission."

Lin smiled faintly.

"It's about etiquette."

Sanna studied the grammar again.

"The structure is polite."

Mateo raised an eyebrow.

"You can tell that from math?"

Sanna nodded.

"Yes."

She pointed to the final segment of the message.

"It includes an uncertainty marker."

Priya was uncomfortable.

"What does that mean?"

Sanna answered simply.

"It's asking."

The room became quiet again.

The network was ancient.

Sophisticated.

And apparently governed by rules.

One of those rules was clear.

New nodes had authority over their own corridors.

Mateo looked at the message again.

"So if we ignore it?"

Lin shrugged.

"Nothing happens."

Priya nodded.

"The corridor remains closed."

Mateo thought for a moment.

Then he asked the obvious question.

"What if we say yes?"

Lin entered the request into the network model.

The simulation ran quickly.

If the relay accepted the request, the corridor geometry would expand.

The gateway would stabilize.

Transit would become possible.

From one star system to another.

In hours.

Priya exhaled slowly.

"That changes everything."

Lin nodded.

"Yes."

She looked around the room.

"For humanity."

The ancient craft docked at the relay remained perfectly still.

Its rings continued rotating slowly, maintaining the corridor's stability.

As if the travelers aboard were waiting for the same answer.

Mateo looked at the message again.

Then he spoke quietly.

"The network welcomed us."

He turned toward the others.

"Maybe it's time we return the courtesy."

Across the solar system, the relay pulsed again.

Seven beats.

Pause.

Seven beats again.

The request remained open.

Waiting.

HALO-1 continued its journey toward the relay, silently recording the unfolding moment.

Humanity's probe would arrive in ninety days.

But the decision about the network could happen long before then.

Priya looked at Lin.

“What do we tell them?”

Lin looked back at the glowing message on the screen.

Then she began typing the first human reply ever sent into the Alignment Network.

Chapter 23: The First Reply

The room had grown very quiet.

On the main display the relay node pulsed steadily in the darkness of the outer solar system. HALO-1 continued its long approach toward the gateway, still months away, while the ancient craft remained docked with the node, its seven rings rotating slowly as they stabilized the corridor.

At the center of the screen the message waited.

REQUEST: NODE ACCESS
ORIGIN: UNKNOWN

Priya looked at Lin.

"Are we really doing this?"

Lin nodded.

"Yes."

Mateo folded his arms.

"History always looks simple after it happens."

Across the secure conference channel scientists from around the world watched silently.

Representatives from

- NASA
- European Space Agency
- Japan Aerospace Exploration Agency
- Indian Space Research Organisation

had joined the session.

The conversation that had begun hours earlier had finally reached its conclusion.

Humanity would answer.

Lin reviewed the message structure one final time.

The Alignment Network did not appear to use conventional language. Every transmission so far had been encoded in mathematical structures that described relationships rather than words.

Coordinates.

State conditions.

Intent markers.

The grammar was elegant.

Universal.

Sanna's voice came through the channel from Helsinki.

"The simplest answer is the correct one."

Lin nodded.

"Yes."

She began constructing the reply.

The message structure appeared on the screen as a sequence of geometric blocks.

Priya leaned closer.

"That's it?"

Lin smiled slightly.

"Yes."

Mateo raised an eyebrow.

"Seems short."

Lin nodded.

"Politeness usually is."

The final message structure appeared.

NODE AUTHORITY: SOL SYSTEM
REQUEST RECEIVED
CORRIDOR ACCESS: PERMITTED

Priya exhaled slowly.

"That's it."

Mateo nodded.

"Send it."

Lin pressed the transmit command.

The message passed through the relay communication channel and entered the gravitational corridor.

For several seconds nothing happened.

The signal simply moved outward along the pathway between stars.

Then the relay responded.

The node pulsed brighter than before.

Seven beats.

Pause.

Seven beats again.

But now the signal carried a new structure layered inside the transmission.

Lin leaned closer to the display.

"That was fast."

Sanna analyzed the response immediately.

Her voice grew quiet.

"It's not from the relay."

Priya considered the implications.

"Then who sent it?"

Sanna rotated the signal geometry.

"It's from the requester."

The message appeared slowly on the screen.

ACCESS GRANTED
TRANSIT CONFIRMED

The room remained silent.

Mateo spoke first.

"So they're coming."

Lin nodded.

"Yes."

Kai adjusted the camera but didn't take the photo immediately.

"People expect the moment to look dramatic," he said to himself.

"It never does."

HALO-1 continued transmitting data from the corridor.

The probe's sensors detected a faint disturbance forming again at the far end of the network connection.

A ripple.

Moving toward the solar system.

Priya watched the model update.

"Something just entered the corridor."

Mateo folded his arms.

"How long?"

Priya finished the calculation.

Her voice dropped slightly.

"Thirty-six hours."

Across the solar system the relay node pulsed again.

Seven beats.

Pause.

Seven beats again.

The corridor between stars had opened fully.

For the first time in human history, humanity had invited a traveler from another civilization to visit.

HALO-1 continued its silent journey toward the gateway.

The probe's cameras remained fixed on the relay and the ancient craft docked beside it.

Recording everything.

Watching as the gravitational corridor carried its next traveler toward the solar system.

Lin looked at the projection of the approaching signal.

Then she said something that made the entire room feel suddenly smaller.

"They answered immediately."

Mateo nodded.

"Which means they were already waiting."

Chapter 24: Emergence

Thirty-six hours passed quickly.

Mission Control remained active around the clock. Scientists rotated through shifts, but no one wanted to leave the room for long. The projection of the solar system remained fixed on the central display, the distant relay node glowing softly in the outer halo beyond Neptune.

The ancient craft remained docked with the node.

Its seven rings continued rotating slowly, maintaining the corridor's alignment.

And somewhere deep along the gravitational pathway, another traveler was approaching.

Priya noticed the first change.

"The corridor just deepened."

Lin looked up immediately.

"What do you mean?"

Priya magnified the curvature model.

The corridor connecting the relay to the distant node had grown stronger, the spacetime gradient becoming steeper near the relay.

Mateo leaned closer.

"That looks like acceleration."

Lin nodded.

"It is."

She pointed to the incoming trajectory.

"The corridor is guiding them in."

HALO-1's sensors began detecting stronger distortions in the corridor geometry.

The probe had moved close enough to the relay that its instruments could observe the gateway directly.

The gravitational field around the node had become complex, layered with multiple curvature structures.

Seven major alignment fields.

Several smaller stabilization zones.

All synchronized.

Across the Atlantic, Sanna studied the signal grammar again.

"The relay is transmitting continuously now."

Priya checked the waveform.

Seven pulses.

Pause.

Seven pulses again.

But now the signal contained a rapid sequence of short transmissions layered inside the pattern.

Lin rotated the signal structure.

"It's traffic coordination."

Mateo smiled slightly.

"Like an airport control tower."

HALO-1 transmitted a new visual frame.

The relay node filled most of the image now.

The structure was enormous—far larger than the probe itself.

A central cylindrical body surrounded by seven curved ring segments, each one extending hundreds of kilometers into space.

The rings glowed faintly with gravitational energy.

Priya whispered,

"That thing has been sitting out there for who knows how long."

Lin nodded.

"Waiting."

The corridor suddenly brightened.

Not with light.

But with distortion.

HALO-1's spacetime sensors recorded a powerful ripple moving along the corridor toward the relay.

The wave passed through the gateway fields like a pulse through water.

Priya's console lit up.

"They're here."

Mission Control fell silent.

The ripple intensified as it approached the relay node.

Then the distortion began to compress.

The corridor geometry folded inward, forming a narrow funnel of curved spacetime directly in front of the gateway.

Lin whispered,

"Transit exit point."

HALO-1's cameras focused on the emerging region.

At first the image showed only the faint glow of distorted stars.

Then something appeared.

A dark silhouette forming inside the corridor.

Slowly resolving against the background of distant galaxies.

Priya leaned closer to the screen.

"That's larger than the first craft."

Mateo nodded.

"Much larger."

The object continued emerging from the corridor.

Not suddenly.

Gradually.

As if slipping out of folded space.

First a long central structure appeared.

Then curved segments extending outward.

Finally the full shape became visible.

Lin stared at the image.

"That's not a ship."

Priya moved closer to the image.

"What do you mean?"

Lin zoomed the projection.

The structure dwarfed the earlier craft that had arrived at the relay.

Its central body stretched several kilometers in length.

Dozens of rotating rings surrounded it, each one producing faint curvature fields.

Mateo said quietly,

"That's a station."

HALO-1's instruments confirmed the scale.

The object was enormous.

More like a mobile corridor hub than a spacecraft.

Its rotating rings stabilized the corridor as it emerged from the gateway.

Sanna examined the relay signal again.

"The grammar changed."

Priya looked up.

"What does it say?"

Sanna translated the pattern.

The message appeared slowly on the screen.

TRANSIT COMPLETE

NETWORK REPRESENTATIVE ARRIVED

The room fell silent again.

Mateo spoke first.

"So they didn't just send a visitor."

Lin took a slow, purposeful breath.

"They sent a delegation."

Outside the relay node, the massive structure completed its emergence from the corridor.

Its rings slowed as the gravitational funnel closed behind it.

The corridor returned to its stable, narrow shape connecting the two star systems.

HALO-1 continued recording everything.

For the first time in human history, humanity had witnessed an interstellar arrival.

Not in the distant future.

Not around another star.

But here.

In the outer darkness of our own solar system.

Priya watched the massive structure slowly maneuver near the relay.

"It's adjusting position."

Lin nodded.

"Probably aligning with the node."

Mateo folded his arms.

"Well."

He looked at the projection of the enormous craft floating beside the gateway.

"I guess they took our invitation seriously."

HALO-1 continued its silent approach.

The probe would reach the relay in less than three months.

But humanity no longer had to wait that long.

The representatives of the Alignment Network had already arrived.

Chapter 25: First Contact

The station stabilized near the relay.

For several minutes nothing happened.

HALO-1 continued transmitting images as the massive structure drifted slowly into position beside the ancient gateway. The two machines—one clearly older, the other far more complex—now floated together in the darkness of the outer solar system.

The corridor behind them remained open.

Stable.

Silent.

Priya monitored the telemetry feed.

"No propulsion signature."

Lin glanced at the data.

"Gravitational control."

Mateo nodded.

"That seems to be their preferred technology."

HALO-1 transmitted another series of images.

The station's design was unlike anything humanity had ever built. Its long central axis extended several kilometers through space, surrounded by concentric rings that rotated at different speeds.

Each ring generated a faint curvature field.

Together they formed a controlled region of bent spacetime.

The structure was not just a vehicle.

It was a **mobile corridor stabilizer**.

Across the secure network link, scientists around the world watched the same images.

Representatives from

- NASA
- European Space Agency
- Japan Aerospace Exploration Agency
- Indian Space Research Organisation

remained connected to the Global Node Council session.

No one wanted to miss what might happen next.

Priya noticed the signal first.

"Lin…"

Lin turned.

"What is it?"

Priya enlarged the waveform display.

"The station is transmitting."

At first the signal looked similar to the relay's pulse pattern.

Seven beats.

Pause.

Seven beats again.

But then a second layer appeared inside the transmission.

More complex.

More structured.

Sanna's voice arrived immediately from Helsinki.

"I see it."

She rotated the signal structure in three dimensions.

"This is different."

Mateo leaned closer.

"How?"

Sanna answered quietly.

"It's not network grammar."

Lin watched the signal model.

"Then what is it?"

Sanna paused for a moment before answering.

"I think…"

She zoomed the waveform.

"It's simplified."

Priya frowned.

"For who?"

Sanna smiled slightly.

"For us."

The message slowly decoded across the screen.

The mathematical structure was no longer purely relational.

It contained recognizable references.

Physical constants.

Atomic transitions.

Distances measured in wavelengths.

The same universal language humanity had used decades earlier on the Voyager probe.

Mateo looked up.

"That can't be a coincidence."

Lin nodded.

"It isn't."

She pointed to the signal.

"They studied us."

HALO-1 transmitted another visual frame.

The massive station remained motionless beside the relay node.

But its rings had changed rotation speed slightly.

As if the structure were carefully adjusting its gravitational field.

The message structure continued resolving.

One symbol appeared repeatedly within the transmission.

Sanna studied it for several seconds.

Then she spoke quietly.

"I think this is a greeting."

The translation engine completed its first rough interpretation.

The words appeared slowly on the screen.

SOL SYSTEM CIVILIZATION

NETWORK ACKNOWLEDGES YOUR NODE

YOU ARE NOT ALONE

No one in Mission Control moved.

For decades scientists had speculated about the possibility of intelligent life beyond Earth.

Now the confirmation appeared calmly on a computer screen.

Mateo finally spoke.

"Well."

He leaned back slightly.

"That answers that question."

The message continued.

More symbols appeared.

More mathematical references.

The grammar remained elegant and precise.

THE ALIGNMENT NETWORK CONNECTS MANY CIVILIZATIONS

YOUR STAR SYSTEM IS NOW ACTIVE

Priya whispered,

"How many?"

Sanna examined the next portion of the signal.

Her eyes widened slightly.

"You might want to sit down for this."

Mateo looked at her.

"That bad?"

Sanna shook her head slowly.

"No."

She zoomed the translation window.

"It's… large."

The next line appeared.

CURRENT ACTIVE NODES: 3,918

Silence filled the room again.

Lin stared at the number.

"That's just this galaxy."

Priya blinked.

"You're sure?"

Lin nodded.

"The signal references spiral arm coordinates."

Mateo folded his arms.

"So nearly four thousand civilizations…"

He looked at the massive station floating beside the relay.

"…and we just joined the club."

The message paused.

Then another segment appeared.

Shorter.

Simpler.

REQUEST: DIALOGUE

HALO-1 continued transmitting images of the station.

The rings rotated slowly.

The corridor remained open.

The network waited.

Lin looked at the message for a long moment.

Then she smiled.

“Well.”

She turned toward the console.

“I suppose we should say hello.”

Chapter 26: The Language Between Minds

The message remained on the screen.

REQUEST: DIALOGUE

Inside Mission Control the room felt strangely calm.

For months the scientists had studied the Alignment Network as an artifact—an ancient technological system spanning the galaxy. Now the network had become something very different.

A conversation partner.

Priya looked at Lin.

"Well?"

Lin smiled faintly.

"I think we should answer."

Mateo leaned back in his chair.

"Carefully."

Across the secure conference channel, specialists from around the world joined the discussion again.

Representatives from

- NASA
- European Space Agency
- Japan Aerospace Exploration Agency
- Indian Space Research Organisation

remained connected to the Global Node Council.

But this time the focus shifted toward one person.

Dr. **Sanna Lehtinen**.

The Finnish linguist had spent her career studying the origins of written language—how early human civilizations had developed the first symbolic systems to represent ideas.

Cuneiform.

Proto-writing.

Mathematical grammar.

Now she was staring at the most sophisticated communication system ever encountered.

"This isn't a language," she said quietly.

"Language is not the goal," Sanna said calmly.

"Shared structure is."

Lin looked up.

"What do you mean?"

Sanna rotated the signal model again.

"It's deeper than language."

Priya leaned forward.

"How?"

Sanna highlighted the mathematical structure embedded in the transmission.

The network did not use words.

It did not even use symbolic meaning in the traditional sense.

Instead, every message described relationships between physical concepts.

Energy.

Distance.

Time.

Topology.

The grammar described **how reality itself was structured**.

Mateo nodded slowly.

"So it's physics."

Sanna smiled.

"Yes."

She tapped the screen.

"Physics used as grammar."

Lin began constructing a reply.

"If we follow the same structure, we can respond."

Sanna nodded.

"That's the idea."

Priya watched as the reply began taking shape.

The message started with a simple declaration.

SOL SYSTEM CIVILIZATION ACKNOWLEDGES NETWORK

Lin added the next element.

A reference to the solar system's position in the galaxy.

A representation of the Sun.

The orbital structure of the planets.

The position of the relay node near the outer halo.

Mateo chuckled quietly.

"We're basically sending them our address."

Sanna added the final portion of the message.

A structural marker indicating dialogue.

A request for mutual exchange of information.

The final message appeared.

SOL SYSTEM CIVILIZATION READY FOR DIALOGUE

Lin looked at the others.

"Send?"

Mateo nodded.

"Send."

The transmission left Earth and passed through the relay node.

From there it entered the corridor connecting the solar system to the larger Alignment Network.

For a moment nothing happened.

Then the station near the relay responded.

HALO-1's instruments detected a sudden increase in signal complexity.

The transmission arriving from the station was far larger than the previous messages.

Sanna frowned.

"That's… interesting."

Priya looked up.

"What is it?"

Sanna rotated the signal geometry again.

"It's not just one sender."

Lin blinked.

"What do you mean?"

Sanna zoomed the waveform.

Then studied the waveform in silence.

"I don't know what it says yet," she admitted.

"But I know what it's doing."

She looked up.
"It's removing ambiguity."

Multiple layers of transmission appeared inside the signal.

Different structures.

Different styles of mathematical grammar.

Mateo leaned closer.

"How many?"

Sanna's voice dropped slightly.

"Several."

Mateo watched the waveform repeat.

"So what are we actually looking at?"

Sanna didn't answer immediately.

"You're asking the wrong question," she said.

Mateo glanced at her.

"Then give me the right one."

Sanna's eyes remained on the pattern.

"Not *what is it*," she said.

"But *what does it assume we already understand*?"

Mateo leaned back slightly.

"That's worse."

Sanna smiled faintly.

"Yes," she said.

"It usually is."

The translation engine began separating the signals.

Each layer carried a different message structure.

But they all shared the same network grammar.

The first decoded message appeared.

WELCOME NEW NODE

A second followed.

OBSERVATION CIVILIZATION IDENTIFIED

A third appeared moments later.

FIRST CONTACT CONFIRMED

Priya stared at the screen.

"That's not just one civilization."

Lin thought for a moment, closed her eyes and shook her head.

"No."

Sanna finished analyzing the signal.

Then she said something that made the room go quiet again.

"They're all listening."

Mateo folded his arms.

"How many?"

Sanna looked back at the earlier network count.

3,918 active nodes.

She smiled slightly.

"Potentially all of them."

HALO-1 continued its silent approach toward the relay.

The probe would arrive in a little over two months.

But humanity was no longer waiting alone in the darkness.

The Alignment Network had begun responding.

And across the spiral arms of the galaxy, thousands of civilizations were now watching Earth.

Chapter 27: The Chorus

The signal did not stop.

After the first three responses appeared, more transmissions followed.

Each one arrived through the relay node in the outer solar system, carried along the same gravitational corridor that had delivered the Network representative station.

The messages did not come all at once.

They arrived in a steady sequence.

Measured.

Orderly.

As if thousands of distant civilizations were taking turns speaking.

Inside Mission Control the translation system began filling the screen with decoded fragments.

WELCOME NEW NODE

A moment later another appeared.

OBSERVATION CONFIRMED

Then another.

NETWORK RECORD UPDATED

Priya stared at the expanding display.

"How many messages are we getting?"

Lin checked the signal stream.

“Dozens so far.”

She paused.

“Possibly hundreds.”

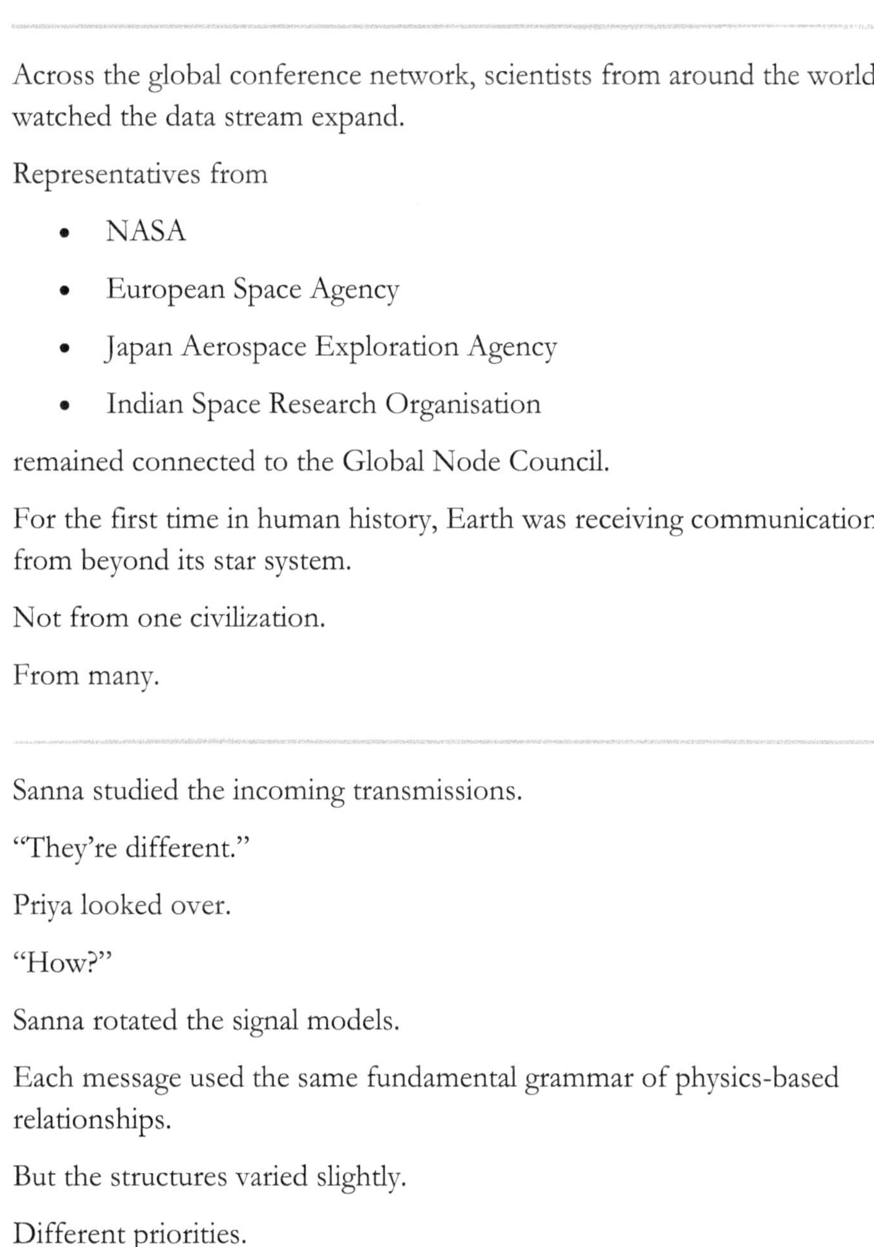

Across the global conference network, scientists from around the world watched the data stream expand.

Representatives from

- NASA
- European Space Agency
- Japan Aerospace Exploration Agency
- Indian Space Research Organisation

remained connected to the Global Node Council.

For the first time in human history, Earth was receiving communication from beyond its star system.

Not from one civilization.

From many.

Sanna studied the incoming transmissions.

“They’re different.”

Priya looked over.

“How?”

Sanna rotated the signal models.

Each message used the same fundamental grammar of physics-based relationships.

But the structures varied slightly.

Different priorities.

Different patterns of emphasis.

Different styles.

"Think of it like accents," she said.

Mateo smiled.

"Alien accents."

Sanna nodded.

"Yes."

HALO-1 transmitted another visual frame of the station near the relay.

The enormous structure remained motionless beside the gateway.

Its rotating rings maintained the corridor's stability as signals continued flowing between the solar system and the wider network.

The station was acting as a communication hub.

A diplomatic relay.

More messages appeared.

Some were short acknowledgments.

Others contained small packets of structured information.

Lin examined one carefully.

"This one includes a star map."

Priya leaned forward.

"Where from?"

Lin zoomed the coordinate grid.

"About six thousand light-years away."

Mateo whistled softly.

"That's quite a neighborhood."

Another message arrived.

Sanna translated the structure slowly.

Her expression changed slightly.

"This one is… interesting."

Priya raised an eyebrow.

"Why?"

Sanna highlighted the final segment.

"It contains a question."

The translation engine processed the grammar.

The message appeared on the screen.

SOL SYSTEM CIVILIZATION

HOW DID YOU FIND THE NETWORK

Mateo chuckled.

"That's a good question."

Lin began assembling the reply.

She included the discovery of the anomaly near the edge of the solar system.

The detection of the relay node.

The arrival of the ancient craft.

And the activation of the gateway.

The reply transmitted through the corridor.

Several minutes passed.

Then the response arrived.

ANOMALY DISCOVERY CONFIRMED

EXPECTED DEVELOPMENT

Priya blinked.

"Expected?"

Lin looked at the signal.

"That's what it says."

Mateo considered the implications carefully and exhaled slowly.

"Expected by who?"

Another message followed immediately.

ALIGNMENT NETWORK OBSERVES EMERGING CIVILIZATIONS

WHEN TECHNOLOGY AND CURIOSITY ALIGN

DISCOVERY OCCURS

The room fell silent again.

Sanna translated the structure slowly.

"They're saying something very specific."

Priya leaned closer.

"What?"

Sanna pointed to the phrase embedded in the message.

"Technology and curiosity."

She smiled slightly.

"That combination seems to be the trigger condition."

Lin looked at the relay node projection.

"So the network doesn't go looking for civilizations."

Sanna shook her head.

"No."

She tapped the screen.

"Civilizations find it."

HALO-1 continued transmitting data as it moved steadily toward the relay.

The probe had become humanity's closest observer of the first interstellar diplomatic encounter.

More messages arrived.

Some simply welcomed Earth to the network.

Others sent small fragments of scientific information.

Mathematical structures.

Astronomical observations.

Hints of technologies far beyond current human capabilities.

Mateo leaned back slowly.

"This is incredible."

Priya nodded.

"It's like opening a library."

Lin studied one of the incoming signals carefully.

"This one is different."

Sanna looked over.

"What does it say?"

Lin enlarged the translation window.

The message was longer than the others.

More complex.

And it originate from a node much closer to the solar system than the rest.

The translation appeared slowly.

SOL SYSTEM CIVILIZATION

YOU HAVE REACTIVATED A VERY OLD NODE

Priya frowned.

"How old?"

The next line appeared.

NODE INACTIVE FOR 3.2 MILLION YEARS

Silence filled the room again.

Mateo spoke quietly.

"So we woke something up."

Lin made a deliberate look. .

"Yes."

The message continued.

THE ALIGNMENT NETWORK HAS BEEN WAITING

HALO-1 drifted onward through the darkness.

The relay node glowed steadily ahead.

Beside it floated the massive station that had come to welcome humanity into the galactic network.

Across thousands of star systems, civilizations were now aware of Earth.

A new voice had joined the chorus.

And the network had begun to speak back.

Chapter 28: The Corridor Equation

The signal arrived quietly.

Among the growing stream of messages flowing through the relay node, one transmission stood out immediately.

It was larger.

Much larger.

Priya noticed it first.

"Lin… you should look at this."

Lin walked over to her console.

"What is it?"

Priya expanded the signal block.

"Data."

Sanna leaned closer to the screen.

"How much?"

Priya blinked.

"About six terabytes so far."

Mateo raised an eyebrow.

"That's not a greeting."

The transmission continued expanding.

Layer after layer of mathematical structures appeared as the relay node passed the information along from the station orbiting beside it.

Sanna rotated the signal geometry slowly.

Her expression shifted from curiosity to something closer to awe.

"This is a research archive."

Lin looked at the expanding model.

"What kind of research?"

Sanna zoomed one of the equations.

Her eyes widened slightly.

"Gravitational topology."

The room grew quiet again.

HALO-1 continued transmitting images of the relay node as the massive station maintained the corridor link. Its rings rotated steadily, stabilizing the pathway between star systems while data flowed along the network.

The station was not just a visitor.

It was acting as a teacher.

Sanna began translating the mathematical structures.

"This civilization is sharing something."

Priya was curious.

"What exactly?"

Sanna highlighted the primary equation.

"It's the corridor field model."

Mateo crossed his arms.

"The one they're using?"

Sanna nodded.

"Yes."

She tapped the screen again.

"And more importantly… how to build one."

Lin stared at the equation.

Even simplified, the structure was enormous.

Dozens of nested tensors described the curvature of spacetime within the corridor.

Energy gradients.

Topology constraints.

Stability conditions.

Mateo exhaled slowly.

“That’s… beyond us.”

Sanna smiled slightly.

“That’s why they simplified it.”

She pointed to a secondary layer in the signal.

“This is the learning sequence.”

The archive was not just a data dump.

It was organized.

Carefully.

The first sections described basic gravitational manipulation.

Later sections introduced corridor stabilization.

And near the end appeared the full model used by the Alignment Network.

Priya stared at the structure.

“They’re teaching us.”

Lin nodded.

“Yes.”

Another signal fragment decoded.

GRAVITATIONAL CORRIDORS ARE NATURAL STRUCTURES

THE NETWORK STABILIZES THEM

Mateo quickly reviewed the previous signals in his mind.

"Natural?"

Sanna rotated the galactic model.

"Yes."

She highlighted the spiral arms of the Milky Way.

The corridors appeared as faint lines connecting regions along the arms.

Not random.

Structured.

Following gravitational gradients within the galaxy itself.

"The spiral arms help guide them," Sanna explained.

"Dense stellar regions create the curvature conditions needed for corridor formation."

Lin studied the spiral arms, then exhaled quickly.

"That explains why the network nodes appear along spiral arms."

Priya leaned back.

"So the galaxy already contains the roads."

Sanna smiled.

"Yes."

She tapped the equation again.

"The network just paved them."

HALO-1 transmitted another image of the station.

The massive rings surrounding the structure rotated slowly, bending spacetime with incredible precision.

Humanity had never built anything remotely like it.

Another message appeared within the archive.

Shorter this time.

More direct.

CORRIDOR ENGINEERING REQUIRES MATURITY

TECHNOLOGY ALONE IS INSUFFICIENT

Mateo raised an eyebrow.

"That sounds philosophical."

Sanna nodded.

"It is."

The next line appeared.

UNSTABLE CIVILIZATIONS DESTROY CORRIDORS

THE NETWORK PROTECTS ITSELF

The room grew quiet again.

Priya spoke softly.

"So access is conditional."

Lin nodded.

"Yes."

She pointed to the earlier message from the network.

"Technology and curiosity."

Mateo added quietly,

"And probably responsibility."

The data archive continued expanding.

More equations appeared.

More models.

More explanations of how spacetime could be manipulated safely.

Lin watched the stream for a long moment.

Then she said something that made the entire room pause.

“If even part of this is correct…”

Priya looked up.

“What?”

Lin pointed to the final section of the archive.

The corridor model expanded outward.

Not just across the galaxy.

Beyond it.

Mateo leaned closer.

“You’re kidding.”

Lin shook her head slowly.

“No.”

She enlarged the model again.

“The Alignment Network isn’t limited to the Milky Way.”

The final line of the archive appeared.

THE NETWORK EXTENDS BETWEEN GALAXIES

HALO-1 continued drifting toward the relay node.

The probe's cameras captured the station and gateway silhouetted against the distant stars.

Humanity had just received its first lesson in interstellar physics.

And the lesson suggested something extraordinary.

The Alignment Network was far larger than anyone had imagined.

Chapter 29: The Builders

The room was quiet except for the faint hum of processors.

On the central display, the galaxy rotated slowly in three dimensions.

Billions of stars.

Hundreds of billions of worlds.

And now, scattered along the sweeping spiral arms, small points of light.

The known Alignment nodes.

Lin Tao stood at the front of the room, studying the map.

"It isn't random," she said.

No one answered.

They already knew.

Priya expanded the projection, overlaying the galactic density map.

Regions of high stellar concentration glowed along the arms like rivers of light.

"Star formation zones," she said. "Density waves moving through the disk."

Mateo nodded.

"Spiral arms aren't fixed structures," he said. "They're gravitational patterns — waves of higher density moving through the galaxy."

Lin pointed to the display.

"And the nodes sit inside those waves."

Priya overlaid another dataset.

Planet distribution.

Heavy element abundance.

Habitable zone estimates.

Every marker clustered along the same sweeping structures.

"The arms contain most of the galaxy's planets," Priya said.

"And most of its chemistry," Lin added.

Hydrogen.

Carbon.

Oxygen.

Silicon.

Iron.

The elements needed for life—and technology.

Mateo leaned forward.

"If you were designing a communication network for intelligent civilizations…"

He gestured toward the spiral arms.

"That's where you'd build it."

Priya zoomed out further.

The map shifted again.

The spiral arms resolved into smooth logarithmic curves.

Arcs expanding outward from the galactic center.

Lin felt a small flicker of recognition.

"Those ratios," she said quietly.

Priya pulled up the data.

The angles between node clusters.

The spacing between relay points.

The curvature of the arms themselves.

The numbers appeared one by one on the screen.

1.618
1.618
1.618

Mateo stared.

"The golden ratio."

Lin nodded.

"Which emerges from the Fibonacci sequence."

She glanced toward the earlier signal recordings.

"The same sequence we detected."

Priya leaned back slowly.

"So the signal wasn't just saying hello."

Lin shook her head.

"No."

She gestured toward the galaxy.

"It was synchronizing with the geometry of the network."

Mateo turned toward the next dataset.

The outer solar system.

The projected position of the relay node near the Oort Cloud.

He highlighted the region.

"Look at where our relay sits."

The display shifted again.

The Sun appeared as a small yellow point.

Beyond it stretched the enormous halo of icy bodies known as the Oort Cloud.

A vast spherical reservoir of comets extending tens of thousands of astronomical units from the Sun.

Priya ran the environmental model.

Solar radiation dropped sharply.

Magnetic interference faded.

Planetary gravitational disturbances diminished.

"Deep quiet," she said.

"The outer halo of a star system."

Lin nodded.

"The perfect place for a relay."

Mateo added another layer.

Gravitational field gradients.

In the inner solar system the map looked chaotic.

Planets.

Orbital resonances.

Perturbations.

But beyond the Kuiper Belt the gradients softened.

Smooth.

Predictable.

Uniform.

Mateo smiled faintly.

"If you wanted to engineer spacetime…"

He pointed to the halo region.

"That's where you'd do it."

For a moment no one spoke.

Then Kai Morgan's quiet voice came from the back of the room.

He had been photographing the screens silently.

"So this isn't just alien technology."

Lin looked at him.

"No," she said.

"It's infrastructure."

Mateo studied the galactic map again.

Civilizations might appear anywhere.

But along the spiral arms they would appear more often.

More stars.

More planets.

More time for intelligence to emerge.

"And when they did," he said slowly, "they would discover the same physics."

Priya nodded.

"They would look for stable gravitational regions."

"Low interference zones."

"Natural geometric alignments."

Lin finished the thought.

"And they would build their node there."

Mateo leaned back.

"A civilization builds a node."

"Another species discovers it centuries later."

"They extend the network."

Priya looked back at the galaxy.

"How long would that take?"

Lin considered the scale.

Millions of years.

Perhaps tens of millions.

Civilizations might rise.

Disappear.

Evolve into something else entirely.

But the network would remain.

Growing slowly across the spiral arms.

Kai lowered his camera.

"So no one civilization built it."

Lin shook her head.

"No."

She looked back at the rotating galaxy.

"It's a cooperative project."

Mateo folded his arms.

"A galactic infrastructure system."

Priya spoke the final thought aloud.

"And we just connected to it."

The galaxy continued its slow rotation on the display.

Billions of stars.

And scattered among them, the quiet lights of the Alignment Network.

Waiting.

The data continued arriving through the relay node.

Equation after equation streamed into Earth's research networks, carried along the gravitational corridor from the station floating beside the gateway.

Most of the information was still far beyond humanity's immediate understanding.

But the structure was clear.

The Alignment Network had not simply appeared.

It had been engineered.

The Global Node Council now met continuously.

Inside a secure facility beneath Geneva, representatives from the world's major space agencies reviewed the incoming data in carefully scheduled sessions. The room itself had been designed for international collaboration: curved screens, multilingual displays, and live feeds from research centers around the planet.

For the first time since the discovery of the relay node, the council was no longer debating what the network was.

They were trying to understand who had built it.

Delegates from

- NASA
- European Space Agency
- Japan Aerospace Exploration Agency
- Indian Space Research Organisation

sat together with astronomers, mathematicians, linguists, and physicists.

Above them the projection of the galaxy rotated slowly.

More than three thousand active nodes glowed along the spiral arms.

Dr. Lin Tao stood near the center of the room.

"We assumed the network was created by a single advanced civilization."

She paused.

"That assumption may be wrong."

Across the world, teams followed the council meeting in real-time.

At the Jet Propulsion Laboratory in California, engineers monitored HALO-1's approach toward the relay node.

In Tokyo, gravitational physics groups examined the corridor equations transmitted by the network station.

In Bangalore, researchers modeled the stability conditions required for corridor construction.

And in Helsinki, Dr. Sanna Lehtinen continued decoding the deeper grammar embedded in the network transmissions.

Sanna rotated the newest dataset on her screen.

"This is not the work of one species."

Priya appeared on the Geneva display.

"What makes you say that?"

Sanna highlighted several sections of the archive.

The mathematical grammar remained consistent.

But the design methods varied.

Some sections described corridor construction using gravitational resonance techniques.

Others relied on extremely precise mass-distribution fields.

Still others used entirely different approaches.

"Different engineering traditions," Sanna explained.

Mateo nodded slowly.

"Like architectural styles."

Sanna smiled.

"Yes."

Lin expanded the network model.

The spiral arms of the Milky Way filled the room.

Thousands of nodes connected star systems across vast distances.

The pattern looked less like a machine and more like an evolving structure.

"Look at the age distribution," Lin said.

Several nodes blinked on the projection.

Each carried a timestamp transmitted within the network archive.

The oldest nodes dated back millions of years.

Others were far younger.

Some have been built within the last hundred thousand years.

Priya leaned forward.

"So civilizations kept adding to it."

Lin nodded.

"Yes."

Mateo crossed his arms.

"It's infrastructure."

The room fell quiet as the realization settled.

The Alignment Network was not a monument built by a single ancient species.

It was a collaborative project.

A system expanded over millions of years as new civilizations joined the network and contributed new nodes.

Priya spoke softly.

"It's like a galactic highway system."

Mateo smiled.

"That's exactly what it is."

Sanna examined another section of the archive.

"This part is interesting."

She enlarged the translation.

The signal grammar contained historical records.

Fragments of network expansion.

Moments when new civilizations had joined and built additional corridor nodes.

Lin read the translated text slowly.

NETWORK EXPANSION IS CONTINUOUS
CIVILIZATIONS CONTRIBUTE NEW CORRIDORS
THE NETWORK GROWS WITH TIME

Mateo leaned back.

"So every civilization that joins eventually helps build it."

Lin nodded.

"Yes."

Priya looked again at the galaxy projection.

"Which means…"

She stopped.

Mateo finished the thought.

"Eventually we will too."

Across the solar system, HALO-1 continued drifting toward the relay node.

The probe had already become one of the most important scientific instruments in human history.

Its cameras recorded the massive station and the ancient gateway working together in perfect alignment.

Two pieces of a structure far larger than humanity had imagined.

Back in Geneva, Lin studied the final portion of the archive.

Another message appeared.

Short.

Ceremonial.

NEW CIVILIZATIONS ARE WELCOMED
WHEN THEY ARE READY

Priya looked up.

"Ready for what?"

Lin pointed to the galaxy map again.

Thousands of glowing nodes stretched across the spiral arms.

Each one a gateway between stars.

Each one a link in the largest engineering project ever attempted.

Lin answered quietly.

"Ready to become builders."

For a moment Lin said nothing.
Then she thought of the silent chamber resting in the deepest trench on Earth — the one built with **seven empty interfaces** waiting patiently in the dark.

"I think," she said quietly, "that was never a lock."

Mateo looked at her.

"It was an invitation."

HALO-1 continued its approach through the darkness beyond Neptune.

The relay node grew slowly larger ahead.

Beside it floated the station sent by the Alignment Network to greet humanity.

A messenger.

A teacher.

And perhaps something more.

Humanity had joined the network.

But the network itself was still expanding.

And somewhere among the distant spiral arms, civilizations had been building it together for millions of years.

Chapter 30: The Second Structure

HALO-1 had been traveling for months.

Now the relay node filled nearly half the probe's forward camera frame.

Beyond the orbit of Neptune, far out in the scattered halo of icy debris surrounding the solar system, the ancient gateway floated silently against the stars.

Its seven arcs rotated with patient precision.

Beside it hovered the massive station that had arrived through the gravitational corridor only days earlier.

Together the two structures formed the first visible outpost of the Alignment Network inside humanity's star system.

HALO-1 transmitted continuous data back toward Earth.

The signal took more than six hours to reach the planet.

By the time the newest telemetry arrived, teams across the world were already waiting.

At the Jet Propulsion Laboratory in California, engineers watched the incoming image frames carefully.

Priya leaned closer to the display.

"Resolution just improved again."

Lin nodded.

"Distance?"

"Two hundred thousand kilometers."

Mateo smiled.

"We're finally getting a proper look."

The relay node was enormous.

Its central cylinder extended several kilometers through space, while the seven curved arcs surrounding it stretched outward like fragments of a ring.

Each arc generated a carefully controlled gravitational field.

Together they stabilized the corridor linking the solar system to distant star systems across the galaxy.

HALO-1's sensors scanned the entire region.

Gravitational fields.

Electromagnetic signatures.

Mass distributions.

Everything looked exactly as expected.

Until something changed.

Priya noticed it first.

"Wait."

Lin turned.

"What?"

Priya enlarged the sensor map.

"There's another object."

Mateo leaned forward.

"Where?"

Priya highlighted the anomaly.

At first it looked like noise in the gravitational field.

But as HALO-1 moved closer, the structure resolved more clearly.

A faint mass signature.

Stationary.

Roughly three hundred kilometers from the relay node.

Lin checked the telemetry.

"That wasn't in the earlier scans."

HALO-1 adjusted its camera orientation.

A new image frame arrived minutes later.

The object appeared at the edge of the field of view.

At first it looked like a cluster of irregular fragments.

But as the probe's optics sharpened the image, the pattern became unmistakable.

Mateo whispered,

"That's not debris."

The structure was enormous.

Not as large as the relay node itself, but still several kilometers across.

Its shape resembled a collapsed ring—sections twisted and broken, as if the structure had once rotated but had long since stopped.

Priya stared at the image.

"That thing has been there a long time."

Lin examined the gravitational readings.

The structure produced no active fields.

No energy emissions.

No rotational stabilization.

"It's dormant," she said.

HALO-1 continued scanning.

The probe's instruments detected something unexpected within the structure.

Residual curvature patterns.

Faint but recognizable.

Mateo's eyes widened.

"Those are corridor alignment signatures."

Priya looked up.

"You mean…"

Lin anticipated the answer.

"Yes."

She magnified the structure again.

The broken arcs surrounding the object matched the geometry of the relay node.

Not identical.

But unmistakably related.

"It's another node."

Silence filled the control room.

Mateo folded his arms.

"So we have two gateways sitting out there."

Lin shook her head.

"No."

She pointed to the damage patterns.

"This one failed."

HALO-1 transmitted additional scans.

Large sections of the structure had fractured long ago.

Some pieces drifted slowly nearby.

Others appeared fused together by ancient impacts.

Priya checked the spectral data.

"The material is similar to the relay."

Lin nodded.

"That confirms it."

Sanna's voice arrived through the conference link.

"I'm seeing the same geometry."

Priya turned toward the screen.

"You recognize it?"

Sanna studied the structure carefully.

"Yes."

She zoomed the pattern.

"This is an earlier design."

Mateo was curious.

"Earlier?"

Sanna nodded.

"The network archive included multiple engineering styles."

She pointed to the twisted arcs.

"This one belongs to an older corridor architecture."

Lin leaned back slowly.

"So before the current relay…"

She paused.

"There was another node."

HALO-1's instruments completed a deeper scan of the dormant structure.

The results appeared seconds later.

Priya read the timestamp estimate aloud.

"Approximately… three point two million years."

The same number that had appeared earlier in the network archive.

The relay node had been inactive for **3.2 million years**.

Mateo exhaled slowly.

"So that's what happened."

Lin nodded.

"The original node failed."

She pointed to the newer relay beside it.

"And the network replaced it."

Priya studied the damaged structure again.

"Why leave the old one?"

Sanna answered quietly.

"History."

HALO-1 drifted closer.

The broken gateway filled the camera frame now.

Ancient metal structures floated in slow motion against the stars.

A relic of an earlier phase of the network.

Then the probe's sensors detected something unexpected.

A faint signal.

Very faint.

But real.

Priya froze.

"Lin…"

Lin leaned forward.

"What is it?"

Priya enlarged the signal waveform.

"It's coming from inside the structure."

Mateo viewed the data, then let out a slow breath.

"That thing has been dead for three million years."

Priya shook her head slowly.

"Apparently not completely."

HALO-1 continued transmitting the signal.

The pattern was weak.

Fragmented.

But recognizable.

Seven pulses.

Pause.

Seven pulses again.

The same pattern used by the relay node.

Back on Earth, the room fell silent again.

Lin stared at the ancient structure.

"Something inside it just woke up."

HALO-1 drifted onward through the darkness of the outer solar system.

Ahead floated the active relay node and the station sent by the Alignment Network.

But now a second mystery had appeared.

A relic from a much older chapter of the network's history.

And something inside it had begun to transmit again.

Chapter 31: The Archive

HALO-1 drifted closer to the ruined structure.

The probe adjusted its trajectory with small bursts from its attitude thrusters, slowly rotating so that its primary sensor array faced the ancient gateway.

The relay node remained active nearby.

Its seven arcs continued rotating in perfect synchronization, maintaining the corridor connection to the Alignment Network.

Beside it, the massive station watched silently.

Neither structure moved toward the ruins.

They simply observed.

Back on Earth, the signal continued repeating.

Seven pulses.

Pause.

Seven pulses again.

But the pattern was unstable.

Fragments appeared between the pulses, like broken pieces of a longer transmission.

Priya isolated the waveform.

"It's not a broadcast."

Lin leaned closer.

"What do you mean?"

Priya expanded the signal structure.

"It's a beacon."

Sanna studied the pattern from Helsinki.

"Yes."

She zoomed the fragments between pulses.

"This was meant to wake up when something approached."

Mateo folded his arms.

"A proximity trigger."

Sanna nodded.

"Exactly."

HALO-1's cameras transmitted the clearest image yet of the ancient node.

Up close, the structure looked older than anything humanity had ever studied.

Large arcs of metallic material had fractured and drifted apart, leaving the central cylinder partially exposed.

Some sections appeared melted.

Others twisted.

The damage had clearly occurred long ago.

Millions of years of micrometeorite impacts had softened the edges of the broken structures.

Dust from the distant Oort Cloud drifted slowly around the ruins.

Priya whispered,

"That thing has been sitting out there longer than humanity has existed."

HALO-1 activated its deep scanning instruments.

Gravitational tomography.

Neutrino density mapping.

Substructure radar.

The probe began constructing a detailed model of the interior.

The signal grew stronger.

The beacon repeated again.

Seven pulses.

Pause.

Seven pulses again.

But now HALO-1 was close enough to identify the source.

Priya's console flashed.

"I have the location."

Lin looked up.

"Inside the core?"

Priya nodded.

"Yes."

HALO-1 transmitted the internal scan.

The ancient node's central cylinder contained multiple chambers.

Most were empty.

Some were filled with fractured machinery.

But one section remained intact.

Perfectly sealed.

Mateo stared at the model.

"That compartment looks… deliberate."

Lin enlarged the structure.

The chamber was small compared to the rest of the node.

Only a few hundred meters across.

Its walls appeared unusually thick.

Like a vault.

Sanna leaned forward.

"That's not part of the corridor mechanism."

Priya looked at Sanna and asked -

"What is it then?"

Sanna answered quietly.

"Storage."

HALO-1 adjusted its sensors again.

The signal clearly originated from within the sealed chamber.

The beacon repeated every twenty seconds.

Still weak.

Still fragmented.

But persistent.

Priya studied the signal fragments carefully.

"There's structure here."

Lin nodded.

"Language?"

Priya shook her head.

"Not exactly."

Sanna rotated the waveform.

"It's compressed."

Mateo raised an eyebrow.

"Compressed what?"

Sanna zoomed the fragments.

The pieces of signal between the pulses began forming recognizable mathematical blocks.

Large ones.

Enormous.

Her voice dropped slightly.

"This is data."

Priya blinked.

"How much?"

Sanna paused.

Then she answered.

"Possibly everything."

Lin stared at the ancient vault.

"You think this is a record?"

Sanna nodded slowly.

"Yes."

She pointed to the signal structure.

"This beacon is announcing the archive."

HALO-1 drifted closer.

The probe's cameras captured the sealed chamber more clearly now.

The outer shell of the vault remained perfectly intact despite the collapse of the surrounding node.

The structure had been designed to survive.

Mateo whispered,

"Three million years…"

Priya nodded.

"And still transmitting."

Lin looked toward the relay node.

The active gateway continued operating normally.

The station sent by the Alignment Network remained nearby.

Watching.

Waiting.

Lin turned back to the vault.

"They knew this might happen."

Sanna nodded.

"Yes."

She pointed to the beacon pattern.

"The archive activates when a new civilization arrives."

HALO-1 completed another scan.

The probe detected multiple layers of encoded information inside the chamber.

Huge volumes of stored data.

Possibly an entire civilization's record.

Priya leaned back slowly.

"That's not just a message."

Lin finished the thought.

"No."

She looked again at the ancient vault drifting beside the ruins of the original relay node.

"That's a library."

HALO-1 continued drifting through the darkness of the outer solar system.

Ahead floated the active relay and the station sent by the Alignment Network.

Beside them lay the broken remains of a gateway built millions of years ago.

Inside it waited the preserved knowledge of a civilization that had once joined the network—and vanished long before humanity ever looked at the stars.

Chapter 32: The First Image

HALO-1 moved carefully around the ancient structure.

The probe's trajectory adjustment thrusters fired in small bursts, positioning the craft within scanning range of the sealed chamber embedded inside the broken relay node.

The beacon continued repeating.

Seven pulses.

Pause.

Seven pulses again.

Now that the probe was close, the fragments between pulses resolved more clearly.

The signal was not random.

It was structured.

Ordered.

Intentional.

Back on Earth the decoding effort expanded rapidly.

Supercomputing clusters across the world began analyzing the signal simultaneously. Research teams at laboratories in California, Europe, Japan, and India worked around the clock, sharing results through the Global Node Council network.

For the first time in human history, scientists were attempting to decode the preserved record of an alien civilization.

Priya studied the compression pattern.

"It's layered."

Lin nodded.

"Multiple archives?"

"Possibly."

Sanna leaned forward from her workstation in Helsinki.

"The structure is similar to the network grammar."

She highlighted several repeating mathematical blocks.

"But simplified."

Mateo frowned and raised an eyebrow.

"Why simplify it?"

Sanna smiled slightly.

"Because whoever built this expected it to be discovered."

HALO-1's instruments detected a secondary transmission embedded within the beacon.

Priya isolated the signal and routed it to the decoding system.

Within seconds the first recognizable structure appeared.

A coordinate grid.

Lin studied it.

"That's a star map."

The grid expanded across the screen.

The structure was immediately recognizable.

It showed the spiral arms of the galaxy.

Thousands of bright points marked locations throughout the Milky Way.

Mateo leaned closer.

"The network nodes."

Lin nodded.

"Yes."

She pointed to one position near the outer edge of the Orion Arm.

"That's us."

Another section of the archive opened.

This one contained a timeline.

Not written in numbers but in cosmic reference points.

Supernova events.

Stellar motions.

Orbital shifts within the galaxy.

Sanna studied the scale.

"This record covers millions of years."

Priya whispered,

"They were documenting their history."

HALO-1 continued scanning the sealed vault.

The probe's sensors detected deeper layers of stored information.

Visual data.

Extensive visual data.

Priya's console lit up.

"I think we have imagery."

The room went quiet.

Lin stared at the images.

"Decode it."

The signal fragments rearranged into a grid.

Pixels began filling the display one by one.

At first the image appeared chaotic.

Bands of light and shadow.

Geometric distortions caused by millions of years of signal degradation.

Then the reconstruction stabilized.

The first clear image emerged.

Mateo exhaled slowly.

"Well…"

The beings in the image were standing in a vast chamber filled with structures similar to the relay node.

Their forms were unlike any life on Earth.

Tall.

Graceful.

Their bodies appeared elongated, supported by multiple flexible limbs that curved outward from a central core.

Their skin—or whatever material covered their bodies—reflected light with a faint iridescent sheen.

Above their central body structures rose several thin sensory appendages that resembled branching antennae.

Priya whispered,

“That’s them.”

The image zoomed outward.

The chamber around them resembled a construction facility.

Sections of corridor rings floated in midair while machines guided them into position.

Workers moved among the structures, assembling the massive arcs that would one day form the gateway network.

Sanna studied the scene carefully.

“They’re engineers.”

Lin nodded.

“Yes.”

She pointed to the rotating arcs.

“They built the first nodes.”

Another image appeared.

This one showed a completed relay structure orbiting a distant star.

The same seven-arc geometry.

The same corridor alignment fields.

Mateo smiled slightly.

"Looks familiar."

The archive continued revealing more images.

Cities.

Star systems.

Massive construction platforms building new nodes along the spiral arms of the galaxy.

Kai adjusted the lens and took a few photos immediately.

"Always expect the moment," he said quietly.

"It's always exciting."

Priya leaned back slowly.

"This civilization helped start the network."

Sanna nodded.

"Yes."

She examined the timeline again.

"The earliest nodes in the archive match their design."

Lin looked toward the projection of the broken relay node drifting beside the active gateway.

"So this was one of their last projects."

HALO-1 continued transmitting the images.

More scenes appeared.

Some showed corridor construction.

Others recorded exploration missions to distant star systems.

Then the tone of the archive changed.

The final images in the sequence appeared darker.

Construction platforms abandoned.

Corridor arcs drifting unfinished in space.

Stars going dark on the network map.

Priya frowned.

"What happened to them?"

Sanna studied the final frames.

"I don't know."

The last image appeared slowly on the screen.

It showed a small group of the alien engineers standing beside a newly completed node.

The gateway arcs glowed softly behind them.

Beyond the structure, the stars of the galaxy stretched across the darkness.

Mateo spoke quietly.

"They look… proud."

Lin nodded.

"Yes."

She looked at the broken relay node again.

"This may have been their last message."

HALO-1 drifted silently between the active gateway and the ancient ruins.

The probe's instruments continued decoding the archive stored inside the sealed vault.

For the first time in human history, humanity was seeing the builders of the Alignment Network.

A civilization that had helped connect thousands of star systems across the galaxy.

And then vanished millions of years ago.

Chapter 33: The Silence

The archive continued unfolding.

HALO-1 maintained its slow orbit around the ruined node while the probe's decoding systems transmitted more fragments of the ancient record back to Earth.

Image sequences.

Engineering diagrams.

Historical timelines.

The builders had documented their civilization carefully.

They had expected someone to find this record someday.

In Geneva, the Global Node Council remained assembled.

The enormous display in the center of the chamber showed the reconstruction of the archive as it expanded across multiple data streams.

Dr. Lin Tao stood near the projection, watching as another segment resolved.

"This part appears to be later in their history."

Priya enlarged the timeline.

The early portions of the archive showed growth.

New nodes built along the spiral arms of the galaxy.

New civilizations joining the Alignment Network.

Construction platforms working continuously.

The network expanding outward.

Then something changed.

Sanna leaned forward from Helsinki.

"The construction rate drops here."

Lin zoomed the data.

Node construction slowed dramatically over several hundred thousand years.

Then stopped entirely.

Mateo narrowed his eyes and thought carefully.

"Why would they stop expanding the network?"

Another image sequence appeared.

This one was darker.

The scene showed the same construction facility seen earlier in the archive—but now the massive corridor rings floated unfinished.

Machines were silent.

Workers were gone.

Priya whispered,

"That place was abandoned."

Sanna translated the accompanying data block.

"It's a record of system failures."

Lin turned toward the display.

"What kind of failures?"

Sanna rotated the signal structure.

"Corridor collapses."

The projection shifted.

Several nodes across the galaxy began blinking red on the map.

Locations where corridors had destabilized.

Collapsed.

Disappeared.

Mateo folded his arms.

"That shouldn't happen."

Lin nodded.

"The equations they gave us show corridors are extremely stable."

Sanna pointed to the anomaly markers.

"These weren't normal failures."

The archive continued.

Another set of images appeared.

Astronomical observations.

Deep-space surveys.

Regions of distorted spacetime far beyond the spiral arms.

Priya studied the star maps.

"These observations are outside the galaxy."

Lin reviewed the deep-space surveys.

"Yes."

The next message decoded.

GRAVITATIONAL DISTURBANCE DETECTED

The archive displayed a simulation.

A massive distortion moving slowly through intergalactic space.

Not a star.

Not a black hole.

Something else.

Mateo stared at the projection.

"What is that?"

Sanna shook her head.

"I don't know."

Another message appeared.

CORRIDOR INSTABILITY INCREASING

NETWORK SAFETY PROTOCOL INITIATED

The simulation expanded.

Corridors across several spiral arms were shut down.

Nodes disconnected.

Entire regions of the network isolated.

Lin spoke quietly.

"They were protecting the system."

Priya zoomed the timeline.

The disturbances continued moving.

Slowly.

Over millions of years.

Mateo hesitated, drawing a slow breath before letting it go.

"So whatever this is… it's traveling between galaxies."

Sanna highlighted the final section of the archive.

"This part is the last entry."

The image appeared slowly.

A group of the alien engineers stood beside the newly completed relay node—the very structure now floating in the outer solar system.

The same image HALO-1 had decoded earlier.

But this time the data block beneath it was complete.

Sanna translated the message carefully.

NODE DEPLOYED

NETWORK LINK STABLE

ARCHIVE PRESERVED

The final line appeared.

WE WILL MONITOR THE DISTURBANCE

The archive ended.

Inside Mission Control no one spoke.

Priya leaned back slowly.

"They left."

Lin nodded.

"Yes."

Mateo looked at the simulation again.

"So they didn't vanish."

Lin shook her head.

"No."

She pointed to the moving distortion outside the galaxy.

"They went to investigate that."

HALO-1 continued drifting between the active relay node and the ancient ruins.

The probe's cameras captured the station sent by the Alignment Network, still maintaining its quiet position beside the gateway.

Then a new transmission arrived from the station.

Short.

Direct.

Lin read it aloud.

ARCHIVE CONFIRMED

THE BUILDERS ARE KNOWN TO THE NETWORK

Priya looked up.

"You mean they're still out there?"

The response arrived seconds later.

STATUS UNKNOWN

The room fell silent again.

Mateo crossed his arms.

"So a civilization that helped build the network…"

He glanced at the broken node drifting outside.

"…went chasing something in intergalactic space three million years ago."

Lin looked concerned.

"Yes."

Priya whispered,

"And never came back."

Far beyond Neptune, the relay node pulsed again.

Seven beats.

Pause.

Seven beats again.

Across the spiral arms of the galaxy, thousands of civilizations remained connected through the Alignment Network.

But somewhere beyond the Milky Way, something had disturbed the corridors themselves.

And the builders of the network had gone to face it.

Chapter 34: The Trajectory

The archive had ended.

For several minutes after the final message appeared, no one in Mission Control spoke. The projection of the galaxy still hovered above the conference chamber in Geneva, its spiral arms glowing with thousands of Alignment Network nodes.

At the edge of the projection, a faint marker indicated the direction of the gravitational disturbance the builders had gone to investigate.

A slow-moving anomaly drifting through intergalactic space.

Three million years ago, the builders had followed it.

And vanished.

HALO-1 continued transmitting data from the outer solar system.

The probe now circled between three structures:

- the active relay node
- the massive Network station
- the broken ruins of the original gateway

The ancient archive vault remained silent now, its beacon finally deactivated after being successfully decoded.

Then a new transmission arrived from the station.

The signal was immediate and deliberate.

Lin noticed the message first.

"This one is addressed directly to us."

Priya enlarged the translation window.

The mathematical grammar resolved quickly.

ARCHIVE INTERPRETATION CORRECT

DISTURBANCE EVENT CONFIRMED

Mateo leaned forward.

"So they know about it."

Sanna studied the signal carefully.

"This message includes observational data."

The display shifted.

A new star map appeared.

Unlike the earlier maps showing the spiral arms of the Milky Way, this projection expanded far beyond the galaxy.

Dozens of nearby galaxies filled the frame.

And between them stretched enormous gravitational currents shaping the large-scale structure of the universe.

Lin was excited and curious.

"This is a cosmological map."

The signal highlighted a region of intergalactic space far beyond the Local Group.

Then the model zoomed inward.

A faint distortion appeared.

A region where spacetime curvature deviated subtly from predicted gravitational flows.

Priya frowned.

"That's the disturbance?"

The station transmitted a confirmation.

YES

Mateo folded his arms.

"That thing must be enormous."

Another message appeared.

SIZE UNKNOWN

STRUCTURE UNKNOWN

Sanna leaned closer to the data.

"They've been tracking it."

The projection expanded again.

A timeline appeared beside the anomaly.

The motion was extremely slow.

Measured in millions of years.

But unmistakable.

The disturbance was moving.

Lin studied the trajectory.

"Heading toward the Milky Way."

The room grew quiet.

Priya performed a quick simulation.

"How long before it arrives?"

Lin ran the numbers.

The answer appeared moments later.

"Approximately eight hundred thousand years."

Mateo exhaled slowly.

"Well… that's not exactly urgent."

Sanna shook her head.

"It might be."

She highlighted a second data layer.

Corridor stability measurements.

Gravitational distortions spreading outward from the anomaly.

"Look at this."

Lin studied the model.

The disturbance did not simply move through space.

It altered the structure of spacetime around it.

Corridor pathways near the anomaly became unstable.

Some collapsed entirely.

Mateo shifted his attention back to the model

"So whatever that thing is…"

Lin finished the thought.

"…it disrupts gravitational corridors."

Priya looked at the galaxy map again.

Thousands of nodes depended on stable corridors to maintain the Alignment Network.

"If that anomaly reached the galaxy…"

Lin nodded.

"Yes."

Mateo spoke quietly.

"It could break the network."

Another message arrived from the station.

THE BUILDERS ATTEMPTED INTERCEPTION

Sanna whispered,

"They tried to stop it."

The next line appeared.

RESULT UNKNOWN

Silence filled the room again.

HALO-1 transmitted a new image of the relay region.

The ancient ruins drifted quietly beside the active node.

The station remained nearby, its massive rings turning slowly as it maintained the corridor connection.

Lin looked at the anomaly projection again.

"Has the network studied it since then?"

The station responded immediately.

CONTINUOUS OBSERVATION

Priya leaned forward.

"And?"

The final message appeared.

DISTURBANCE CONTINUES TO MOVE

The projection of the galaxy rotated slowly above the council chamber.

Across the spiral arms, thousands of civilizations remained connected through the Alignment Network.

For millions of years the system had functioned as the backbone of interstellar travel and communication.

But something far beyond the galaxy had begun disturbing the structure of spacetime itself.

And it was still coming.

HALO-1 drifted silently through the darkness beyond Neptune.

The probe's cameras recorded the relay node, the Network station, and the ancient ruins.

Three pieces of a much larger story.

A story that had begun millions of years before humanity looked toward the stars.

And might one day involve them as well.

Chapter 35: The Advantage

The projection of the anomaly remained suspended above the council chamber in Geneva.

A faint distortion drifting slowly through the darkness between galaxies.

According to the Network station, the phenomenon had been observed for millions of years. Its motion was steady, predictable, and extremely slow.

Eight hundred thousand years remained before it would reach the outer gravitational domain of the Milky Way.

By human standards, the threat was distant.

But by galactic standards, it was already underway.

HALO-1 continued transmitting observations from the relay region beyond Neptune.

The probe now maintained a stable orbit between the active gateway and the ancient ruins of the earlier node.

The Network station remained nearby.

Its massive rings rotated slowly, maintaining the corridor link to the wider Alignment Network.

Inside Mission Control the data streams continued expanding.

Astronomers began comparing the disturbance with known cosmic phenomena.

Dark matter flows.

Rogue black holes.

Gravitational waves from distant galaxy mergers.

None of the models matched perfectly.

Priya stared at the anomaly simulation.

"It's not behaving like a massive object."

Lin nodded.

"No."

She rotated the spacetime model.

"It behaves more like a distortion moving through the fabric itself."

Mateo leaned back.

"A wave?"

Lin shook her head.

"Not exactly."

Sanna spoke from Helsinki.

"It might be topology."

Everyone turned toward her.

Priya raised an eyebrow.

"Topology of spacetime?"

Sanna nodded.

"Yes."

She enlarged the disturbance model.

"Imagine spacetime as a fabric with folds and tensions. If a large-scale distortion moves through that fabric, it can alter the geometry everywhere along its path."

Mateo smiled faintly.

"So corridors collapse because the underlying geometry changes."

Lin nodded.

"That would explain everything."

The station transmitted another message.

NETWORK ANALYSIS CONSISTENT WITH YOUR INTERPRETATION

Priya blinked.

"Well… that's encouraging."

Another message followed immediately.

This one was longer.

More deliberate.

THE DISTURBANCE IS DIFFICULT TO STUDY

Lin frowned.

"Why?"

The station responded.

OBSERVATION DISTANCE IS GREAT

MEASUREMENT UNCERTAINTY IS HIGH

Sanna leaned forward.

"You're not learning their language," she said.

"You're learning how they think reality is structured."

"They're too far away."

The station transmitted again.

YES

The message paused.

Then a second block of text appeared.

YOUR STAR SYSTEM IS UNIQUELY POSITIONED

Mateo raised an eyebrow.

"That sounds promising."

Priya enlarged the galactic model.

The Milky Way appeared again, its spiral arms stretching outward.

The solar system's position near the outer edge of the Orion Arm was highlighted.

Lin studied the geometry.

Then she understood.

"We're ahead of it."

The disturbance was moving toward the Milky Way from intergalactic space.

The solar system happened to sit directly along the projected entry region where the distortion would first begin affecting the galaxy.

Priya nodded slowly.

"We're the closest network node to its path."

The station confirmed.

CORRECT

Sanna smiled slightly.

"So we can observe it before anyone else."

Another message appeared.

EARLY OBSERVATION IS CRITICAL

Mateo crossed his arms.

"For what?"

The station answered.

UNDERSTANDING THE DISTURBANCE

MAY REQUIRE NEW PHYSICS

The room grew quiet.

Lin looked at the anomaly again.

"So the builders weren't just chasing it."

Sanna nodded.

"They were trying to understand it."

The station transmitted one final message.

THE NETWORK INVITES YOUR CIVILIZATION

TO PARTICIPATE IN THIS STUDY

Priya leaned back slowly.

"That's quite an invitation."

Mateo smiled.

"We've been part of the network for about two days…"

He gestured toward the projection of the galaxy.

"…and they're already giving us a research project."

Lin watched the relay node glowing softly on the screen.

The ancient gateway.

The ruins of the earlier node.

The station sent by the Alignment Network.

For millions of years the network had expanded across the galaxy, connecting thousands of civilizations through gravitational corridors.

Now humanity had joined that system.

And the network had given them their first responsibility.

Lin spoke quietly.

"Well."

She looked again at the anomaly drifting through the darkness between galaxies.

"Let's start observing."

HALO-1 continued its silent orbit beyond Neptune.

The probe's sensors scanned the relay region, the ancient ruins, and the vast emptiness of the outer solar system.

Somewhere far beyond the Milky Way, spacetime itself was slowly shifting.

And for the first time, humanity had a chance to study it.

Chapter 36: The Observatory

The proposal arrived less than two hours after the invitation.

Inside Mission Control the first collaborative design packet transmitted from the Network station appeared on the central display.

It was not a message.

It was a blueprint.

Priya enlarged the data block.

"That's… a lot of math."

Mateo smiled.

"That seems to be their preferred language."

Sanna studied the structure.

"They're proposing an observatory."

Lin leaned forward.

"Where?"

Sanna highlighted the coordinates embedded in the design.

The model expanded into a three-dimensional projection of the outer solar system.

Neptune's orbit appeared first.

Beyond it stretched the scattered disk and the distant halo of icy bodies surrounding the Sun.

And at the center of the model floated the relay node.

Priya nodded.

"They want to build it here."

The simulation expanded further.

Additional points appeared throughout the outer solar system.

Each point represented a potential instrument location.

Together they formed an enormous geometric array.

Mateo stared at the model.

"That's not an observatory."

Lin smiled.

"It's a detector."

The Network station transmitted another explanation.

THE DISTURBANCE ALTERES SPACETIME TOPOLOGY

DIRECT OBSERVATION REQUIRES LARGE BASELINES

Sanna translated quietly.

"They need distance between sensors."

Priya rotated the model.

The outer solar system provided exactly that.

Distances of billions of kilometers.

Perfect for detecting extremely subtle gravitational distortions.

Lin thought for a moment, then let out a slow deliberate breath.

"This could work."

HALO-1 appeared in the model as the first instrument.

The probe already carried extremely sensitive gravitational sensors designed for navigation and anomaly detection.

Those sensors could be repurposed.

Mateo chuckled.

"So our little probe just became part of the galaxy's largest experiment."

The Network design packet added additional components.

Autonomous sensor platforms placed along distant heliocentric orbits.

Small gravitational reference stations.

Corridor calibration beacons.

Priya zoomed the projection.

"How many instruments are they suggesting?"

Lin read the design summary.

"Forty-two."

Mateo raised an eyebrow.

"That's… specific."

Sanna smiled slightly.

"The number corresponds to the geometry of the relay node."

Lin pointed to the projection.

The instruments would form a massive ring around the Sun.

A gravitational interferometer spanning the entire outer solar system.

Priya leaned back slowly.

"That's incredible."

The station transmitted again.

INITIAL DEPLOYMENT CAN BEGIN WITH EXISTING PROBE

HALO-1 appeared highlighted in the model.

Mateo nodded.

"Phase one is already out there."

Another message followed.

NETWORK WILL PROVIDE ADDITIONAL SENSOR NODES

Lin blinked.

"They're sending equipment."

The simulation updated again.

Additional stations would arrive through the gravitational corridor.

Compact instruments designed to anchor themselves within stable solar orbits.

Each one carrying sensors far more sensitive than anything humanity had built.

Priya laughed softly.

"So they're helping us build the experiment."

Sanna studied the final section of the design packet.

"The data architecture is interesting."

Lin looked up.

"How so?"

Sanna highlighted the relay node.

"All measurements feed into the node."

The relay acted as the central processor for the entire observatory.

Data from every sensor would converge there before being distributed across the Alignment Network.

Mateo folded his arms.

"That thing is basically a galactic supercomputer."

HALO-1 transmitted another image of the relay region.

The ancient gateway glowed softly against the distant stars.

The massive Network station continued rotating beside it.

Beyond them drifted the ruins of the earlier node and the sealed archive vault.

Three million years of history floating together in the darkness.

Lin studied the observatory model again.

"This will allow us to detect the disturbance long before it reaches the galaxy."

Sanna nodded.

"And understand what it actually is."

The station transmitted one final message.

THE BUILDERS BEGAN THIS STUDY

YOUR CIVILIZATION MAY CONTINUE IT

The words hung quietly on the screen.

Priya leaned back.

"That's quite a legacy."

Lin smiled.

"Yes."

She looked again at the projection of the solar system observatory forming across billions of kilometers of space.

"And quite a responsibility."

Far beyond Neptune, HALO-1 adjusted its orbit slightly.

The probe's sensors continued scanning the relay region as the first instrument of the Solar System Gravitational Observatory.

Somewhere in intergalactic space, the disturbance continued moving.

Slowly.

Inevitably.

And for the first time in the history of the Alignment Network, a newly joined civilization had begun helping to study it.

Chapter 37: Arrival

HALO-1 crossed the final hundred kilometers slowly.

The probe's navigation thrusters fired in brief pulses, adjusting its trajectory as it approached the relay node for the first time.

For months the gateway had been a distant shape in its cameras.

Now it filled the sky.

Back on Earth, the control rooms watching the mission had grown quiet again.

At the Jet Propulsion Laboratory, Priya leaned forward in her chair as the newest image arrived.

"Distance?"

Lin glanced at the telemetry.

"Eighty-three kilometers."

Mateo smiled faintly.

"We made it."

The relay node towered above the probe.

Up close the structure was even larger than earlier estimates suggested. The central cylinder stretched nearly four kilometers from end to end, while the seven great arcs surrounding it curved outward in elegant segments of metallic geometry.

Each arc rotated slowly.

Not mechanically.

Gravitationally.

Their motion was silent, guided by fields bending spacetime itself.

HALO-1 transmitted its first high-resolution panorama of the gateway.

The images arrived on Earth minutes later.

Engineers and scientists across the world watched as the ancient machine revealed its details.

Fine lattice structures supporting the arcs.

Thousands of sensor nodes embedded across the surface.

Energy channels running through the central cylinder like veins of dim blue light.

Priya whispered,

"It's beautiful."

Mateo nodded.

"It's engineering art."

The probe drifted beneath the nearest arc.

HALO-1's instruments recorded the gravitational curvature fields in exquisite detail.

The structure produced a stable region of bent spacetime several hundred kilometers across.

The corridor connection to the Alignment Network ran through the center of that field.

Invisible.

But very real.

Lin studied the data.

"The equations they sent us match perfectly."

Sanna's voice arrived through the network link from Helsinki.

"That confirms the archive."

HALO-1 continued its inspection orbit.

The probe passed along the length of the central cylinder, its cameras capturing features never seen before.

Engraved structures.

Symbols.

Not words.

But geometric patterns embedded into the surface of the machine.

Priya enlarged one of the images.

"That looks deliberate."

Sanna analyzed the pattern.

"These are network markers."

Lin tilted her head.

"Like signatures?"

Sanna nodded.

"Yes."

She zoomed the pattern.

Each arc carried slightly different geometric markings.

Different engineering styles.

Mateo smiled.

"Multiple builders."

The discovery matched what the archive had already suggested.

The relay node had not been built by one civilization.

It had been expanded and maintained by many.

A shared structure evolving across millions of years.

HALO-1 rotated slowly toward the far side of the gateway.

The Network station floated nearby.

From this distance the station looked enormous—its rotating rings forming a complex gravitational structure that helped stabilize the corridor.

The station transmitted a greeting.

HALO-1 PROBE

ARRIVAL CONFIRMED

Priya laughed softly.

"They know its name."

Lin nodded.

"We introduced ourselves."

Another message appeared.

PROBE MAY APPROACH STATION

Mateo folded his arms.

"That sounds like an invitation."

HALO-1 adjusted its orbit again.

The probe's trajectory shifted slightly, bringing it closer to the massive station.

The structure was unlike anything humanity had built.

Its central axis stretched nearly ten kilometers in length.

Dozens of rotating rings surrounded it, each generating precise gravitational fields used to control corridor geometry.

Priya watched the camera feed.

"That's not just a station."

Lin nodded.

"It's a mobile node."

The station could move between relay locations across the network, stabilizing corridors and assisting with large-scale engineering projects.

A traveling piece of the Alignment Network itself.

HALO-1 approached slowly.

The probe's cameras captured the surface of the station in extraordinary detail.

Smooth structures.

Field generators.

Observation ports embedded into the outer rings.

Mateo leaned closer to the screen.

"Do you see that?"

Priya zoomed the image.

Along one section of the station's outer ring was a large transparent structure.

Inside it, faint shapes moved.

Lin stared at the display, trying to understand what she was seeing.

"That's… not machinery."

Sanna spoke quietly.

"No."

The translation system began processing the station's next transmission.

REPRESENTATIVES REQUEST DIRECT OBSERVATION OF YOUR PROBE

Priya blinked.

"They want to look at HALO-1."

Mateo chuckled.

"Fair enough."

HALO-1 drifted closer to the station.

Inside the observation chamber the faint figures became clearer.

Several tall, slender forms moved slowly within the chamber, their elongated bodies reflecting the light of the distant Sun.

The first living beings humanity had ever seen from another civilization.

The probe continued transmitting images back to Earth.

For the first time in human history, humanity was looking directly at intelligent life from another star system.

HALO-1 floated quietly beside the station.

The relay node glowed softly behind it.

The ancient ruins drifted farther away in the darkness.

Three million years after the builders had left their archive behind, a new civilization had arrived at the gateway.

And the network had welcomed them.

Chapter 38: The First Exchange

HALO-1 floated quietly beside the station.

The probe's small body—no larger than a compact satellite—drifted slowly along the outer perimeter of the massive structure. The rotating rings of the station moved with patient precision, bending spacetime with subtle gravitational fields that kept the corridor stable behind them.

Inside the observation chamber, several figures stood watching.

For a moment neither side transmitted anything.

Both civilizations were simply observing.

Back on Earth, the control room had become silent.

Every major space agency remained connected through the Global Node Council network.

Scientists, engineers, and diplomats from

- NASA
- European Space Agency
- Japan Aerospace Exploration Agency
- Indian Space Research Organisation

watched the same images as they arrived from the edge of the solar system.

Six hours earlier, HALO-1 had captured the first glimpse of the Network representatives.

Now the probe's cameras resolved them clearly.

Several additional national and private observatories were believed to be monitoring the signal independently.

The beings inside the observation chamber moved with deliberate grace.

Their bodies were tall and elongated, supported by several flexible limbs that curved outward from a central structure. The limbs were capable of fine manipulation as well as locomotion.

Their skin—or outer surface—reflected light softly with faint iridescent patterns.

Above the central body rose several slender sensory appendages that extended and shifted gently as they examined the probe.

Priya whispered,

"They're studying it."

Lin nodded.

"So are we."

HALO-1 slowly rotated so that its primary imaging system faced the observation chamber directly.

The probe had no eyes.

But its camera array captured every detail.

Inside the chamber, one of the figures stepped closer to the transparent barrier.

The being extended one of its flexible limbs toward the probe.

The motion was slow.

Careful.

Quite curious.

Mateo smiled faintly.

"That looks familiar."

Priya raised an eyebrow.

"What do you mean?"

Mateo shrugged.

"It looks exactly like what a human scientist would do."

Sanna studied the posture.

"Yes."

She nodded slightly.

"That's curiosity."

The station transmitted a new message.

VISUAL EXCHANGE CONFIRMED

Lin responded immediately through the relay.

HUMANITY GREETS YOU

The reply transmitted through the gravitational corridor and reached the station moments later.

Inside the observation chamber the figures shifted slightly as if acknowledging the signal.

Another message arrived.

WE GREET YOUR CIVILIZATION

Priya exhaled slowly.

"Well."

Mateo leaned back in his chair.

"That makes it official."

HALO-1 continued transmitting high-resolution images of the chamber.

The representatives were examining the probe carefully, moving around the viewing area as they observed its structure.

One of them manipulated a small device attached to the chamber wall.

The station transmitted again.

YOUR PROBE IS ELEGANTLY DESIGNED

Priya laughed softly.

"I'll take that as a compliment."

Lin smiled.

"Yes."

She typed the response.

THANK YOU

IT WAS BUILT TO EXPLORE

The station responded quickly.

EXPLORATION IS A COMMON TRAIT

Sanna read the message quietly.

"Among civilizations that join the network."

HALO-1 drifted slightly closer to the observation chamber.

From this distance the representatives could clearly see the probe's antenna arrays, sensor modules, and maneuvering thrusters.

And the probe could see them.

For the first time in history, humanity and another intelligent species were looking directly at each other across space.

Not through telescopes.

Not through radio signals.

But face to face.

The relay node glowed softly behind the station.

Seven arcs rotating slowly.

Seven pulses repeating through the network.

Lin watched the screen for a long moment.

Then she said quietly,

"I think this is the beginning of something very important."

HALO-1 floated peacefully beside the station.

Beyond it stretched the vastness of the solar system.

Beyond that, the spiral arms of the Milky Way.

And beyond those, the darkness between galaxies where the disturbance continued its slow journey.

But for the moment, two civilizations had simply stopped to meet.

Chapter 39: The Builders' Path

HALO-1 continued its quiet orbit beside the station.

The probe's cameras transmitted a steady stream of images back toward Earth: the relay node glowing softly behind the station, the broken ruins of the earlier gateway drifting farther away, and the distant stars stretching across the dark halo of the outer solar system.

Inside the observation chamber, the representatives of the Alignment Network still watched the small human probe with evident curiosity.

For a while the transmissions between the station and Earth remained simple.

Greetings.

Basic scientific exchanges.

Shared astronomical observations.

Two civilizations learning how to speak to each other.

Then the station transmitted something new.

The signal was larger than the earlier conversational messages.

Lin noticed it first.

"This is a data archive."

Priya enlarged the transmission window.

"From the network?"

Sanna examined the structure.

"Yes."

She rotated the signal model.

"But it's not general information."

Mateo leaned closer.

"What is it?"

Sanna answered quietly.

"It's about the builders."

The room grew still.

The projection above the council chamber shifted.

The galaxy appeared again.

Thousands of glowing nodes stretched along the spiral arms of the Milky Way.

Then the map zoomed outward.

Beyond the galaxy.

Into the vast darkness between galaxies.

A path appeared.

A faint line beginning near the Milky Way and extending outward into intergalactic space.

Lin studied the trajectory.

"That's their route."

Priya nodded slowly.

"The builders followed the disturbance."

The station transmitted confirmation.

THE CIVILIZATION YOU CALL THE BUILDERS

JOINED THE NETWORK 6.4 MILLION YEARS AGO

Another message followed.

THEY CONTRIBUTED MANY EARLY NODES

Sanna smiled faintly.

"That matches the archive."

The station continued.

THE DISTURBANCE WAS FIRST DETECTED BY THEIR ASTRONOMERS

The projection shifted again.

The anomaly appeared far beyond the Milky Way.

A subtle distortion moving slowly through intergalactic space.

Mateo followed the signal pattern across the monitor.

The signal repeated.
The pattern held—long enough to rule out coincidence.
And then the system responded.

"They discovered it first."

Lin nodded.

"And they decided to investigate."

The station transmitted another sequence of images.

These were older than anything HALO-1 had discovered in the archive.

Massive vessels.

Not small ships.

Entire fleets.

Structures large enough to carry entire populations.

Priya whispered,

"That's an expedition."

Sanna translated the next message.

THE BUILDERS ORGANIZED A LONG-DURATION MISSION

The timeline appeared beside the images.

Millions of years.

Mateo leaned back slowly.

"They weren't planning to come back anytime soon."

Lin nodded.

"No."

She pointed to the enormous vessels drifting away from the galaxy in the simulation.

"They were leaving."

The station transmitted the final part of the record.

THEIR FLEET FOLLOWED THE DISTURBANCE

IN ORDER TO UNDERSTAND IT

The simulation ended.

The fleet vanished into the darkness beyond the Milky Way.

Silence filled the room again.

Priya spoke softly.

"So they chased the mystery."

Lin nodded.

"Yes."

Sanna looked at the anomaly projection again.

"And no one has heard from them since."

The station transmitted another message.

THE NETWORK CONTINUES TO MONITOR THE DISTURBANCE

Mateo folded his arms.

"Has anyone else tried to follow them?"

The station paused for several seconds before replying.

NO CIVILIZATION HAS YET ATTEMPTED SUCH A MISSION

Lin raised an eyebrow.

"Why not?"

The answer arrived slowly.

THE DISTANCES ARE IMMENSE

THE RISK IS UNKNOWN

Priya smiled faintly.

"Fair enough."

HALO-1 continued drifting beside the station.

The probe's cameras captured the relay node glowing quietly against the distant stars.

Three million years earlier the builders had left an archive here before departing on their mission.

A message for whoever came next.

Lin studied the projection of the builders' path.

The faint line stretching from the Milky Way into intergalactic space.

Mateo looked at her.

"You're thinking about it."

Lin smiled slightly.

"Yes."

Priya shook her head.

"We just joined the network yesterday."

Lin laughed.

"That's true."

But she kept looking at the map.

Somewhere in the darkness beyond the galaxy, a civilization that helped build the Alignment Network had vanished while studying the greatest mystery in the universe.

And now a new civilization had arrived at the gateway they left behind.

HALO-1 floated quietly beside the station.

The first human probe ever to reach the threshold of the galactic network.

Watching.

Learning.

And perhaps someday…

Following the path the builders had taken millions of years before.

Chapter 40: The Question

The map of intergalactic space remained suspended above the council chamber.

A thin line extended from the Milky Way outward into the darkness beyond.

The route taken by the builders' expedition.

Millions of years ago they had left the galaxy to study the disturbance moving through intergalactic space.

And they had never returned.

For a long time, no one spoke.

The room was filled with the quiet hum of computers processing the immense volume of data arriving through the relay node.

Outside the windows of the Geneva facility the lights of the city glowed softly along the edge of Lake Geneva.

Inside, humanity considered its place in a much larger story.

Priya broke the silence.

"So what happens now?"

Lin looked at the projection.

"That's the question."

HALO-1 continued orbiting near the relay node far beyond Neptune.

The probe's sensors recorded the gateway, the Network station, and the distant ruins of the earlier node.

For months the small spacecraft had been humanity's eyes at the threshold of the Alignment Network.

Now it had become something else.

The first representative of Earth in interstellar space.

The Network station transmitted another message.

YOUR CIVILIZATION HAS ENTERED THE NETWORK

A second message followed.

MOST NEW CIVILIZATIONS REQUIRE TIME TO ADAPT

Mateo smiled.

"That sounds reasonable."

The message continued.

SOME CIVILIZATIONS CHOOSE TO EXPLORE

Lin raised an eyebrow.

"Some."

The projection changed again.

This time the station displayed examples of early network exploration missions conducted by other civilizations after joining the Alignment Network.

Small scientific expeditions.

Survey probes.

Occasionally large research vessels.

Sanna studied the pattern.

"They all started the same way."

Priya leaned closer.

"With probes."

The station confirmed.

AUTONOMOUS MISSIONS ARE COMMON FIRST STEPS

Mateo folded his arms.

"That sounds familiar."

Lin glanced toward the HALO-1 telemetry feed.

"Our probe already crossed the threshold."

The station transmitted again.

HALO-1 HAS DEMONSTRATED SUCCESSFUL TRANSIT STABILITY

Priya blinked.

"Transit?"

Lin looked up.

"They mean the corridor."

HALO-1 had not traveled through the gravitational corridor yet.

But its sensors had measured the stability of the pathway connecting the relay node to distant star systems.

The probe had proven that human technology could safely operate near the gateway.

Another message appeared.

THE NETWORK CAN SUPPORT FURTHER MISSIONS

Mateo leaned back.

"That sounds suspiciously like encouragement."

Sanna smiled.

"Yes."

The station transmitted one final message.

DOES YOUR CIVILIZATION INTEND TO EXPLORE BEYOND ITS STAR SYSTEM

The question hung quietly in the room.

Priya looked around the council chamber.

"That's not a small decision."

Lin nodded.

"No."

Mateo smiled faintly.

"But it's the right question."

Across the planet the discussion began immediately.

Scientists.

Engineers.

Political leaders.

Philosophers.

Humanity had just joined a network connecting thousands of civilizations across the galaxy.

Now the network had asked the obvious question.

Would Earth remain a distant observer?

Or would humanity begin exploring the galaxy itself?

HALO-1 continued drifting quietly beside the station.

The relay node pulsed behind it.

Seven arcs turning slowly in the darkness.

Seven pulses repeating across the Alignment Network.

Three million years earlier the builders had left the Milky Way in pursuit of a mystery moving through intergalactic space.

Now a new civilization had reached the gateway they left behind.

And the galaxy was waiting to see what humanity would do next.

Chapter 41: First Step

The decision did not come quickly.

For weeks the Global Node Council met in nearly continuous sessions. Scientists presented proposals, engineers outlined technical challenges, and diplomats debated the implications of sending humanity's first official mission beyond the solar system.

The Alignment Network station remained patient.

It did not pressure the new civilization.

It simply waited.

Meanwhile, HALO-1 continued its quiet orbit beside the relay node.

The probe had become a symbol of humanity's first step into the larger universe. Its sensors fed constant streams of data into the newly forming Solar System Gravitational Observatory.

Forty-two sensor platforms were now under construction on Earth, each designed to be deployed through the network corridor and placed into distant solar orbits.

The observatory would watch the disturbance for generations.

But the question before the council was different.

The network had asked something much larger.

Would humanity explore?

Priya stood near the central display in Geneva.

"I think we already answered that question."

Mateo smiled slightly.

"How?"

Priya pointed to the telemetry feed from HALO-1.

"We built that probe."

Lin nodded.

"Exploration is already part of who we are."

Sanna joined the conversation from Helsinki.

"For thousands of years humans crossed oceans simply because they wanted to know what was on the other side."

She paused.

"The corridor is just a larger ocean."

The station transmitted a message.

NETWORK READY TO SUPPORT TRANSIT

The room grew quiet again.

Lin turned toward the council.

"We don't need to send people yet."

Priya nodded.

"Start with another probe."

Mateo chuckled.

"That seems to be a popular strategy."

The plan formed quickly.

A second-generation probe would be built.

Small.

Highly autonomous.

Equipped with gravitational sensors, astronomical instruments, and communication arrays capable of operating through the network.

Its mission would be simple.

Travel through the corridor.

Visit nearby nodes.

Return knowledge.

The council voted.

The decision was unanimous.

Humanity would explore.

Three months later, the new probe arrived at the relay node.

HALO-1 watched from its orbit as the vehicle drifted slowly toward the corridor.

The station remained nearby.

Inside the observation chamber, the representatives watched as well.

The probe aligned itself with the center of the relay arcs.

Gravitational fields stabilized.

The corridor brightened slightly as spacetime folded inward.

Priya watched the telemetry stream in silence.

Mateo folded his arms.

Lin counted down quietly.

"Three…
Two…
One…"

The probe slipped into the corridor.

For a brief moment its signal stretched across the curved geometry of the gateway.

Then it vanished.

The transmission reappeared seconds later.

From another star system.

Priya smiled.

"It worked."

Mateo laughed softly.

"Well."

He looked around the room.

"I guess humanity just became an interstellar civilization."

HALO-1 continued orbiting the relay node.

The ancient gateway glowed softly against the distant stars.

Three million years earlier the builders had left an archive here.

A message for whoever came next.

Now someone had answered.

Chapter 42: The Long Future

The Solar System Gravitational Observatory grew slowly.

Over the following years new instruments arrived through the corridor network.

Some were built on Earth.

Others were provided by civilizations already connected to the Alignment Network.

Together they formed an immense scientific array spanning billions of kilometers across the outer solar system.

HALO-1 remained the oldest instrument in the system.

The probe had become a historical artifact as well as a working scientific platform.

Its cameras still drifted quietly through the relay region, recording the ancient gateway and the station that had welcomed humanity to the network.

The disturbance continued moving through intergalactic space.

Slowly.

Imperceptibly.

But now it was being studied by thousands of civilizations working together across the galaxy.

Every day new data flowed through the network.

Astronomical observations.

Physics models.

Engineering ideas.

The shared knowledge of countless worlds.

Humanity contributed its own discoveries.

New approaches to gravitational sensing.

Improved corridor stabilization algorithms.

Better models of spacetime topology.

The Solar System Observatory became one of the most important research sites in the Alignment Network.

But sometimes the scientists working late at night would look at the projection of the galaxy and think about something else.

The builders.

Somewhere far beyond the Milky Way, a civilization that helped construct the Alignment Network had vanished while studying the disturbance.

Their path still stretched across the star maps like a faint line leading into the darkness.

Priya once asked the station a question.

"Do you think they are still out there?"

The station answered simply.

UNKNOWN

But then it added something else.

THE NETWORK CONTINUES THEIR WORK

HALO-1 drifted quietly beside the relay node.

The probe's sensors recorded the slow rotation of the gateway arcs.

Seven segments turning in perfect harmony.

Seven pulses repeating through the network.

Across the spiral arms of the Milky Way, thousands of civilizations remained connected by the corridors.

Some explored.

Some built new nodes.

Some studied the deep mysteries of the universe.

And one small blue world near the edge of the Orion Arm had just begun its journey among them.

The relay pulsed again.

Seven beats.

Pause.

Seven beats again.

Mateo studied the projection of the Alignment Network in silence.

Lines of faint light stretched across the galaxy, linking stars separated by distances impossible to comprehend.

"All this time," Mateo said quietly, "we thought we were trying to understand the signal."

He shook his head slightly.

"But the signal wasn't the discovery."

He looked around the room.

"The discovery is that civilizations eventually stop building alone."

The door opened quietly behind them.

Kai Morgan stepped inside, a small camera resting in his hand.

He paused for a moment, studying the projection that now connected humanity to a network millions of years in the making.

Without speaking, he lifted the camera and took a single photograph.

Kai lowered the camera.

"History doesn't feel like history when you're inside it," he said.

The signal spread across the network—crossing distances no human system had ever bridged in real time.

Far beyond the galaxy, spacetime shifted quietly as the disturbance continued its long journey through the cosmos.

Somewhere ahead of it—perhaps millions of years away—the builders might still be watching.

And somewhere beyond the edge of the galaxy, another civilization may one day look back and recognize the moment humanity joined the conversation.

The network had always been there.

Humanity had not discovered it.

Humanity had finally reached the point where it could be seen.

Late that evening, a brief message appeared in the shared network logs.

Somewhere in the South Atlantic, near the South Sandwich Islands, a survey vessel had reported something unusual on the ocean floor.

The coordinates were still being verified.

But the message had already begun circulating through the network.

ATHENA flagged the report less than three seconds after it entered the system.

End of *The Alignment Echo III: The Alignment Network*

The network had been waiting.

Now it was growing again.

Postscript: The Alignment Network

The Alignment Network may not have been built by a single civilization.

Across the spiral arms of the Milky Way, thousands of relay nodes connect distant star systems through carefully engineered gravitational corridors. Some of these nodes are ancient beyond measurement. Others are newly constructed by civilizations that have only recently joined the network.

No surviving archive identifies a single origin.

Instead, the evidence suggests something far more remarkable.

Over millions of years, many civilizations contributed to the network's expansion—each adding new corridors, new relay nodes, and new discoveries. What began as isolated experiments in gravitational engineering gradually became a shared cosmic infrastructure.

A collaboration spanning the galaxy.

Humanity joined this network only recently.

Our first probe crossed the relay near the edge of our solar system and returned knowledge that will shape our understanding of the universe for generations.

What lies beyond the Milky Way—and what became of the ancient builders who followed the great disturbance into intergalactic space—remains unknown.

But the network continues to grow.

Civilization by civilization.

Discovery by discovery.

And now humanity has taken its first step.

Our chapter has only just begun.

Far beyond the Milky Way's spiral arms, in the deep darkness between galaxies, a faint disturbance moved silently through intergalactic space.

The Alignment Network had noticed it long ago.

Its sensors had been watching for millions of years.

The disturbance was growing stronger now.

And somewhere across the vast web of nodes, a signal quietly changed priority.

A new civilization had joined the builders.

The network would soon need them.

Appendix: Global Considerations

Global Node Council

Formed after the discovery of the Alignment Network, the Global Node Council coordinates humanity's scientific, engineering, and diplomatic response to the interstellar infrastructure discovered beyond the solar system.

The council includes representatives from major space agencies and scientific institutions around the world.

The response to the discovery involved cooperation among several major international space agencies, including NASA, the European Space Agency (ESA), the Japan Aerospace Exploration Agency (JAXA), and the Indian Space Research Organisation (ISRO).

Together these organizations coordinate humanity's first missions into the gravitational corridor network.

Other major spacefaring nations were closely monitoring developments and conducting independent analyses. These included the China National Space Administration (CNSA) and the Russian space agency Roscosmos, both of which possess significant deep-space observational capabilities and scientific expertise.

While not formally part of the initial response coalition described in this report, these organizations represent important participants in the broader global scientific community responding to the discovery.

Artificial Systems

HALO-1

Autonomous deep-space probe designed to explore the relay node discovered near the edge of the solar system. HALO-1 becomes humanity's first representative within the Alignment Network and provides the first images of the relay station and its inhabitants.

Solar System Gravitational Observatory

A distributed network of gravitational sensors deployed across the outer solar system to monitor the mysterious spacetime disturbance approaching the Milky Way.

The Alignment Network

Relay Node (Solar Halo Node)

An ancient gravitational gateway located near the outer boundary of the solar system. The node serves as a connection point between the solar system and the larger Alignment Network spanning the Milky Way.

The Network Station

A monitoring and coordination platform maintained by civilizations already connected to the Alignment Network. The station oversees corridor stability, node maintenance, and communication between participating species.

The Builders

An ancient civilization that helped construct early portions of the Alignment Network millions of years ago.

Records discovered within the relay archive indicate that the builders were among the first to detect the mysterious intergalactic disturbance currently being studied by the network. Their expedition followed the anomaly into deep intergalactic space.

Their ultimate fate remains unknown.

The Alignment Network Civilizations

Thousands of civilizations across the Milky Way participate in the Alignment Network, contributing to the construction and maintenance of gravitational corridors linking distant star systems.

Many of these civilizations share scientific knowledge through the network's communication infrastructure.

Only a small number have been directly encountered by humanity so far.

The Disturbance

A vast spacetime anomaly moving slowly through intergalactic space toward the Milky Way.

The disturbance was first detected millions of years ago and appears to be the central mystery that inspired the creation of the Alignment Network.

Understanding its nature has become one of the network's most important scientific goals.

Humanity

The newest civilization to join the Alignment Network.

Having only recently discovered the gravitational corridor near the edge of the solar system, humanity now stands at the threshold of a much larger cosmic community.

Its first steps into the network may determine its role in the long future of the galaxy.

About the Author

Mark Anderson, PhD writes science-driven fiction at the intersection of artificial intelligence, discovery, language, and the future of human decision-making. His stories explore how curiosity, responsibility, and imagination shape the path of emerging technology and humanity's place in a wider universe.

When not writing fiction, he works in AI, regulatory science, and medical technology, bringing real-world scientific thinking into speculative storytelling grounded in possibility rather than fantasy.

He is the author of **The Alignment Echo trilogy** and continues to explore connected stories about discovery, choice, and the systems we build to understand the unknown.

Short About the Author

Mark Anderson, PhD writes science-driven fiction exploring artificial intelligence, discovery, and humanity's place in a larger universe. Drawing on his work in AI, regulatory science, and medical technology, he creates speculative stories grounded in real scientific ideas. He is the author of *The Alignment Echo* trilogy.

Back Cover Copy

The Alignment Echo III

Humanity has identified an ancient relay near the edge of the Oort Cloud. It is part of the Alignment Network—gravitational pathways linking civilizations across the Milky Way.

Some are still active.
Some have gone dark.

HALO-1, humanity's most advanced probe, is sent to investigate.

What it finds changes everything:
Velocity unchanged.
Distance decreasing.

Space itself is not fixed.

The network has been shaping spacetime—creating corridors where distance collapses and travel follows the curvature of reality.

Humanity discovers the universe itself has been engineered for travel

Some civilizations are participants.
A few became builders.

Long ago, one of the first builders left the galaxy…
and never returned.

The anomaly they pursued is now heading toward us.

Humanity has been given a choice:

join the network—
or help build what comes next.

Description

The Alignment Echo III

The Alignment Echo III is a science fiction novel exploring humanity's first encounter with an advanced interstellar system embedded within the fabric of spacetime.

After identifying an ancient relay near the edge of the Oort Cloud, scientists discover that it is part of the Alignment Network—a system of gravitational pathways linking civilizations across the Milky Way. Some of these pathways remain active, while others have gone dark over time.

When the deep-space probe HALO-1 is sent to investigate, it records an unexpected physical phenomenon: velocity remains constant while distance decreases. This observation reveals that space itself is not fixed. Instead, the network has been shaping spacetime, creating corridors where distance collapses and travel follows the **natural** curvature of reality.

Within this network, civilizations take on different roles. Some are participants, using the pathways for exploration and connection. Others have become builders, contributing to the construction and expansion of the system.

Humanity discovers the universe itself has been engineered for travel

Historical records suggest that one of the earliest builder civilizations left the galaxy in pursuit of an unidentified anomaly and never returned. That same anomaly is now approaching the Milky Way.

Blending elements of astrophysics, artificial intelligence, and speculative cosmology, The Alignment Echo III presents a scientifically grounded vision of interstellar travel, first contact, and the evolving role of humanity in a structured universe. The novel explores themes of discovery, responsibility, and the choice between participation and creation within a larger cosmic system.

The Seven Keys

Across the Alignment Network, relay nodes are often constructed with seven primary interfaces.

No surviving archive identifies the original designers of this system, and the meaning of the seven-key architecture is debated among many civilizations.

Some believe it is purely functional — a stable configuration for coordinating gravitational corridor alignment.

Others believe it carries symbolic meaning.

Seven has appeared repeatedly across many cultures throughout history, long before those civilizations understood the structure of the universe around them.

Seven directions of motion in complex spacetime models.
Seven layers of orbital resonance in early network construction.
Seven synchronization intervals required to stabilize a corridor between distant stars.

Whether by design or coincidence, the pattern persists.

The first relay discovered by humanity also required seven keys.

And when the system activated, it revealed something extraordinary:

No civilization opens the network alone.

The Alignment Network was never meant to belong to a single species.

It was meant to grow.

Civilization by civilization.
Discovery by discovery.

Seven keys.

And always one more hand reaching toward the next door.

The network was not built to be completed.

It was built to continue.

More Books by Mark Anderson, PhD

Speculative Fiction & Thoughtful Science

The Alignment Echo I II & III (Series)
A science-driven trilogy exploring discovery, artificial intelligence, and humanity's place in a much larger universe. Beginning with a mysterious deep-space signal and expanding into a vast interstellar network, the series asks a timeless question:

Is intelligence something that speaks — or something that knows when not to?

The Observatory at the Edge of Time (coming soon)
After *The Alignment Echo.*

Artificial Intelligence & Technology

Does AI Scare You? Yes. No. Maybe.
A thoughtful and accessible exploration of artificial intelligence, examining both the promise and the concerns surrounding rapidly advancing technology. Rather than fear or hype, the book invites readers to approach AI with curiosity, critical thinking, and a deeper understanding of how intelligent systems are shaping the future.

Children & Adult Bilingual Adventures

Tommi the Green Tomato (Series)
Playful, imaginative stories about curiosity, friendship, and growing wiser. Tommi's adventures combine humor, language learning, and gentle philosophical moments, encouraging young readers to explore the world with open minds and kind hearts. Bilingual in several languages.

Creative Cooking & Everyday Intelligence

The Accidental Genius & Snackcidents
Practical, inventive cooking built around real ingredients and real hunger. These books celebrate simple foods—beans, grains, vegetables, and everyday creativity—showing how curiosity in the kitchen can turn ordinary meals into satisfying discoveries.

Cook & Cancer
Practical, outstanding cooking built around meal and soup recipes. The book celebrates easy to make home cook foods for someone special.

Not the end. The beginning of alignment.

www.ingramcontent.com/pod-product-compliance
Lightning Source LLC
LaVergne TN
LVHW010638110826
845149LV00014B/2880

* 9 7 9 8 9 9 4 9 3 5 7 6 7 *